FOSSIL COVE PRESS

THE BEAR CAVALRY

The True (Not!) History of the Icelandic Bears

by

D. G. Valdron

FOSSIL COVE PRESS
1301 - 90 Garry Street, Wpg, Man, Canada, R3C 4J4

THE BEAR CAVALRY
The True (Not!) History of the Icelandic Bears
By D.G. Valdron

Cover: Christopher Martinez, artist. TheChristopherMartinez.com

Issued in print and electronic formats
ISBN: (pbk) 978-1-998453-23-8
ISBN: (ebook) 978-0-9879061-7-5

THE BEAR CAVALRY

A True (Not!) History of the Icelandic Bears

Table of Contents

Introduction

This probably isn't what you were expecting. Sorry about that.

What you were probably anticipating was some thundering badass novel about badass Vikings charging down on some unsuspecting medieval village, riding badass Grizzly bears.

Well, that happens.

Sort of.

As awesome as it is, the notion of Bear Cavalry is utterly ridiculous. Trying to saddle up ole Bruin is a good way to get dismembered, and in particularly messy ways.

But I like a challenge. In this case, how would you even get domesticated bears? And once domesticated, what utter lunatic would think it a good idea to try and ride one make them into a (fearsome) cavalry force. So I cracked the books, researched, read, and figured I'd found a reasonably plausible pathway. A historical 'might have been.'

But that seemed pretty dry. So I imagined and visualized it as a fun, funky 'Super Size Me' style documentary, and tried to write it down as if the you were watching it on your television screen, rather than just reading it.

I was pretty happy with it. I hope you will find it entertaining, or at least… unique.

So, here's 'Bear Cavalry' the totally not true (but could have been) history of the fighting bears of Iceland.

As to the Sharebear Apocalypse, I realized I'd written a pretty fun story in a very similar format. It's a fairly savage take on a beloved children's cartoon series.

It's also inspired somewhat by the raccoons my dad raised from infancy (kittency?), and by remarkable ways that humans can be stubborn in the face of apparent facts – modern politics as the example.

The two seem to belong together.

You who are about to read, I salute you. Good luck!

ONWORD

The Bear Cavalry
The True (Not!) History of the Icelandic Bear

OPENING MONTAGE - The Danish Royal Bear Cavalry in procession; Rembrandt's famous 'Ragnarok' featuring Norse Gods mounted on Bears, black and white footage of bear cavalry circa 1914 moving jerkily, a series of impressionistic paintings, Teddy Roosevelt riding a bear up San Juan Hill, Vikings on Bears, clips of mounted Bear Brawls, the animals rearing up to club each other, faux woodcuts of Vikings riding bears fighting horse mounted nights.

ROBIN PRUFROCK - VOICE OVER: Is there anything more awesome than Bear Cavalry! I think I was nine years old when I watched Teddy Roosevelt charge up San Juan Hill on a giant Grizzly Bear on our new color TV.

INSERT: John Bodine, Director of 'The Rough Riders, The Teddy Roosevelt Story' "....this wasn't in the script at all. In real life, it was a straightforward cavalry charge, he was riding a horse. But the word came down from the studio heads 'Make it BIGGER! He should be riding a Bull Moose!' Well, we managed to get a bull moose, but no one could get near the damned thing despite it being supposedly tamed. So there we were, a week behind schedule, shooting everything else but the scene and trying to figure out how to dress up a horse to look like a moose, when one of the P.A.'s, some Icelandic girl, she said 'Why don't you get a bear? We ride them all the time back home.' Well, it turned out that the Danish Bear Guard was in Canada, by coincidence... And that was it, the rest is history. I think that's the most famous scene I ever shot..."

INSERT FILM CLIP OF THE ROUGH RIDERS: The actor playing Teddy Roosevelt leaps atop an obviously stuffed Grizzly bear, followed by shots of a stuntman riding a bear up the hill, and close ups of the actor rocking back and forth on the stuffed bear, waving a cavalry saber.

CUT BACK TO - Interview with Bodine: That wasn't John of course. Can you imagine what the studio would have done if we'd let our star get near a bear. We didn't use our own stuntman, we had one of the Danes do it, dressed him up to look like John. I remember, he was a small man, maybe five feet. It made the bear look positively gigantic. We had to be really careful, no explosions, no gunshots, not even horses... they would just panic. But we got the shot, and it looked damned good!

INSERT BRIEF CLIP of the actor playing Teddy Roosevelt giving a Rebel Yell.

CUT TO PRUFROCK: We all grew up on this stuff. Vikings and Bears. I mean, you had to be tough to ride a bear, right?

MONTAGE: Gary Larson cartoons, Tom of Finland drawings of leather men on Bears, excerpt from 'Blazing Saddles' of Mongo riding a Bear into down, excerpts from the sword-and-sandals flick 'Hercules and the Vikings' etc. Mounted bears rearing and grappling, while their riders punched and swung at each other. Home movie footage of younger children riding piggyback on older children, grappling. B-movie and documentary footage.

ROBIN PRUFROCK VOICE OVER: Bear cavalry, bear riders, Vikings and bears, the knights on horses versus bears and Vikings, it was a part of our culture's visual language. I remember my little brother riding on my back, holding on, while we played 'Viking Battles.' Then, I don't know... We all kind of grow up and move on. Bears are cool, but it doesn't matter much when you've got a nine to five. These days, we all drive cars. And as it turns out a lot of this stuff was... shall we say... exaggerated.

CUT TO: Old man in a museum, caption reads: "Wilfred Hyde Pierce. Historian, Middle Ages"

WILFRED HYDE-PIERCE: Vikings versus Knights? (Chuckles) That never happened. Yes, there were Vikings and Norsemen, and yes, some of them rode bears. And yes, there were certainly knights. And during the Norse invasions, yes, there was certainly a lot of fighting. But you absolutely never ever saw a confrontation between a mounted knight on a horse and a Norseman on a bear. (Chuckles again) A bear! Do you see one of them sitting still for the long sea voyage to France on a Viking long ship. I should say not. This is just the movies, and while movies are noted for their historical accuracy, in this case they've got it wrong.... mostly....

CUT TO ROBIN PRUFROCK: No San Juan hill? No Vikings versus Knights? Bummer. Was there anything to it at all? Was it just some great big cultural hoax? Actually, there's a real story, a remarkable story. We start with the Vikings....

CLOSE UP OF PRUFROCK GRINNING - From the very beginning, the Vikings were into bears.

CUT TO: A gay disco, huge, fat, grinning, hirsute, long haired, bearded men wearing leather vests and thongs are dancing. One wearing a horned helmet, and holding an improbably huge stein of beer looks directly at the camera, flashes an even bigger smile, and gives a thumbs up.

VO PRUFROCK: Not that kind of Bear! Well, that too, I suppose. But mainly....

CUT TO: CLOSE UP - URSUS HORRIBILIS - A GIANT GRIZZLY BEAR REARS ON ITS HIND LEGS AND ROARS AT THE CAMERA.

PRUFROCK (VOICE OVER): This kind.

****

INTERVIEW SHOT, PRUFROCK AND TOM HAGGERTY, ANTHROPOLOGIST (NAME IN SUBTITLES)

TOM HAGGERTY- It was about the environment. The Norse occupied Scandinavia. There wasn't a lot in the way of big predators up there. Down in southern regions, you had tigers in Asia, lions in the middle east and Africa, leopards, crocodiles. Most of these animals were not native to Europe, but only known through trade, Europeans had a pretty good idea of what they were and what they represented. There was a lot of symbolism, a lot of baggage, which accumulates around Lions for instance, to the point where German or English Lords in countries which weren't within a thousand miles of lions had them on the heraldry.

But Scandinavia was something of a backwater. It was so remote that lions and tigers really didn't have much of an impact. They weren't even folklore. Instead, when the Norse were looking around for something big and dangerous, well, they naturally turned to the European Brown Bear, the biggest, baddest most dangerous animal in its environment, much larger and stronger than wolves....

PRUFROCK: But it goes back even further than that, doesn't it?

MONTAGE - Excepts from B&W 'One Million BC', primitive ape men fighting cave bears. Clips of Bear skinned shamans dancing around a fire. Shots of the Lascaux cave paintings. Museum exhibits of cave bears.

TOM HAGGERTY, VOICE OVER: Certainly, Bear worship and veneration in Europe probably goes all the way back to the Neanderthal, and the battles with cave bears. Bears have always symbolized power and strength. They are immensely strong animals, they can stand upright like we do, they have a similar diet to us, and they liked to shelter in the same caves we wanted. There wasn't that much distance separating early man from early bears, except that bears were bigger, stronger and hairier.

QUICK SHOT: Gay 'bear' in thong and Viking helmet grins and 'thumbs up' the camera.

TOM HAGGERTY: Any society which found itself living actively in close quarters with bears was going to venerate them. Certainly the Native Americans did. And the Norse were no different. You have to remember that the Norse prior to 800 CE were really a marginal European culture. They were living in an area where agriculture was fairly borderline, there was a lot of difficult geography, hills, fjords, you couldn't go in and clear-cut it for fields. You were farming, you were herding, you were doing hunting and fishing. It was untamed land, and untamable land, and it was definitely bear country. This countryside offered a lot of shelter for bears, a lot of hunting and fishing opportunities. So you had the Norse living side by side with bears in a way that just wasn't happening anywhere else in Europe.

PRUFROCK: Side by side, eh?

TOM HAGGERTY: (laughs) Not peaceably, god no! You basically have two species occupying the same territories and they're both big adaptable predators. A lot of bears got killed by Vikings. A lot of Vikings got eaten by bears. Sometimes they left each other alone, or kept out of each others ways, but when they didn't.....

TOM HAGGERTY: Anyway, Bears acquired this mystique for Norse, for power and ferocity. Something that they were encountering first hand. This is where you got Berserkers. Literally - it means 'Bear Shirt' - These were men who would literally channel the ferocious fighting spirit and strength of Bears, originally, putting on Bear skin or Bear shirt as a kind of totemic magic.

PRUFROCK: I thought they were just battle crazed fighters.

TOM: Definitely, they were that. But I think it's pretty clear that the earliest incarnations were shamanic conjurers. They were literally becoming bears, letting the spirit of bears fill them. Over time of course it just generalizes to battle ferocity. But even then, there is a direct reference to the Bear as the inspiration. They fight like bears; they are as strong as a bear. The Bear as an iconic symbol really gets entrenched in Norse culture.

PRUFROCK: They even made pets of them.

TOM HAGGERTY: Indeed yes, there was a time during the Viking age when Bears as pets were almost common. It was a huge status symbol for a chieftain or a lord or a king to keep a bear as a pet. It was common enough that in Scandinavia jurisdictions passed laws basically prohibiting people from antagonizing pet bears or their owners.

PRUFROCK: Excuse me. I think if someone owns a bear for a pet, the last thing you'd want to do is antagonize them. It's a bear. It stands upright seven feet tall. It can take the head off a bull with one swipe. Poodles are nasty enough to antagonize, but bears? What are they thinking?

TOM HAGGERTY: Mostly (chuckles) they weren't thinking I suppose. This is a culture which thought having brown bears as pets was a good idea. Let's take it for granted that there was a lot of bad judgement going around.

PRUFROCK: But these weren't domesticated yet, were they?

TOM HAGGERTY: Correct. Brown bears were never domesticated, they were tamed. There's a big difference between domesticated and tame, between dogs and wolves. These were wild bears, raised as cubs and tamed. That's what the Norse did. They would take cubs and raise them up.

PRUFROCK: Did that work?

TOM HAGGERTY: To an extent. Cubs were always fun, playful. There's a lot of reports everywhere of people raising bear cubs. The Indians did it, the British did it.... that's where Winnie the Pooh comes from, an actual bear cub raised by an army unit. That's where we get Smokey the Bear, again a bear cub rescued after a forest fire.

PRUFROCK: Sure, everyone loves the cubs, they're easy to handle, they're fun to have around. But then they grow up...

TOM HAGGERTY: Yes, they grow up.

PRUFROCK: What happens then?

TOM HAGGERTY: Well, they reach sexual maturity, become sexually active, they get older, wild instincts reassert, they get more dangerous. Adolescent bears are okay. Even young bears are okay. But some of them, as they get older and crankier, they get more dangerous. Even mild mannered, they're dangerous, they're immensely strong animals, and they have huge claws. They can do damage without meaning to. And if they intend to do damage, watch out...

PRUFROCK: That doesn't sound good.

TOM HAGGERTY: We don't have a lot of records as to the outcomes with bears raised as pets, but I would venture that they probably aren't good. Some of them probably returned to the wild. Some probably ended up causing a lot of death and damage or needing to be put down. A lot probably ended up in cages or chained up. And they got expensive, this is a seven hundred pound meat eater after all....

PRUFROCK: That's a lot of hamburger.

TOM HAGGERTY: Certainly.

PRUFROCK: So the whole pet bear thing, it was basically on its way to being just a fad...

TOM HAGGERTY: Precisely.

CUT TO MONTAGE: Black and white clips, hula hoops, sock hops, exotic flying machines....

PRUFROCK: So what happened?

CUT TO A MAP OF EUROPE, CENTERED ON SCANDINAVIA - ANIMATION

WILFRED HYDE WHITE - VOICE OVER - "The Viking Age!"

****

The Bear Cavalry — Page 11

ROBIN PRUFROCK STANDS ON THE BUSY CITY SQUARE IN COPENHAGEN IN FRONT OF A STATUE OF HANS CHRISTIAN ANDERSON'S 'LITTLE MERMAID',

HE IS DRESSED AS A HOLLYWOOD VERSION OF A VIKING WARRIOR, WITH A HELMET BORROWED FROM RAPPER FLAVA FLAV.

BEHIND HIM THE SWEDISH BIKINI TEAM JOGS PAST, CIRCLING BEHIND THE FOUNTAIN AND BACK ACROSS THE CAMERA AGAIN.

ZOOM IN ON PRUFROCK, WHO GRINS AT THE CAMERA.

PRUFROCK: Around the beginning of the 9th century, something was taking place in the world. It was getting warmer. This was the medieval warm period, and it coincides almost exactly with the great era of the Viking raids. What happened was that when things started to warm up, it began to warm up in the north first. For the Norsemen, living in pretty marginal areas, life began to get easier.

CUT TO: Climatologist Jeff Oblast (name and occupation in subtitles), in his office, surrounded by maps and charts.

JEFF OBLAST: What was going on is that the environment is getting warmer at higher and higher latitudes and elevations, your growing season is getting longer. Suddenly, you're growing much better and bigger crops. Crops that couldn't even grow in Scandinavia are moving north. You're cultivating Barley near the arctic circle. It's not just crops - warmer temperatures, longer growing seasons mean that cattle are getting more forage, so they're growing faster and larger, they're reproducing faster, giving more milk. Even the forests are affected, you're seeing rapid growth in tree rings, and consequently better denser woods.

CUT BACK TO: PRUFROCK FLIRTING WITH THE BIKINI TEAM, ONE OF WHOM IS NOW WEARING FLAVA FLAV'S FAUX VIKING HELMET. HE LOOKS UP AT THE CAMERA.

PRUFROCK: Warmer temperatures meant life was getting better for the Norse. More food, better food, less work, more relaxation, more fun (grins) and what do people like to do when they're having fun....

CUT TO A GRAPHIC OF SCANDINAVIA - 8 BIT GRAPHICS OF NORSE MEN AND WOMEN HOLDING HANDS DOT THE GRAPHIC. BIG GRINS POP UP ALL OVER ON THE FACES OF THE NORSE MEN AND WOMEN.

PRUFROCK VOICE OVER: .... And nine months later....

CUT TO GRAPHIC: NORSE MEN AND WOMEN BEGIN TO MULTIPLY, POPPING UP ALL OVER THE PLACE TO CUTE LITTLE SOUND BLIPS, FASTER AND FASTER UNTIL THE MAP OF SCANDINAVIA IS COVERED WITH PROLIFERATING NORSE.

CUT TO PRUFROCK

PRUFROCK: There is a population boom, and suddenly, there's an overpopulation. Too many Norse men, too many Norse women, and more coming all the time. So what do they do? They go sailing, looking for new real estate...

CUT TO HISTORIAN WILFRED HYDE WHITE: It is the most extraordinary thing. Without warning, without precedent, this sleepy little corner of Europe explodes. The Vikings are on the move and they are literally bursting across

Europe, terrorizing all these states and societies that really have no idea how to cope with them.

CUT TO: POV OF PROW OF A VIKING SHIP, THE DRAGON MASTHEAD APPARENT. AS THE FOG CLEARS, STARTLED VILLAGERS LOOK UP ALL ALONG THE SHORE AND START TO RUN.

CUT TO PRUFROCK

PRUFROCK: The Norse had learned to build long ships to travel and fish in the fierce Atlantic waters. But now, they found that these ships could carry them almost anywhere. The Norse became perhaps the greatest sailors of the pre-modern world, traveling further than almost anyone.

CUT TO: CGI MAP OF EUROPE, A SUCCESSION OF ARROWS EXTENDING OUT OF SCANDINAVIA IN ALL DIRECTIONS.

PRUFROCK VOICE OVER: They raided Scotland, then England, then Cornwall and Wales and Ireland. They raided Normandy and Bretton and France. The established kingdoms, some transient, some which endured.

They sailed even further south, raiding the coasts of what is now Spain and Portugal, pushing all the way to Morocco...

They entered the Mediterranean, raided North Africa and Sicily, captured slaves all along the coast of Europe and sold them in Morocco and the Barbary coasts.

They sailed north into the Baltic sea, and then into the Arctic Ocean and the Barents Sea, hugging coasts and following rivers into the heart of what is now Russian territory. Up the Volga River. Into Belarus and Ukraine, they formed the state that would eventually evolve into Russia.

Following those rivers further south, dragging their ships overland from one waterway to the other, they made it all the way into the Black and the Caspian Seas, encountering the Byzantine and Persian Empires, and reaching as far as Baghdad..

In Constantinople, they wowed the locals with their strength and ferocity, and were hired on becoming the Varangian Guards.

They explored, they fought, they killed and plundered. Sometimes they traded. Sometimes they stayed, setting up shop in their new homes.

From about 850 through to 1150, the Norse were literally unstoppable. They simply went where they wanted, and no one, no one was able to resist.

CGI MAP PROLIFERATES WITH GRAPHICS OF LONG SHIPS AND VIKINGS, ARROWS EVERYWHERE, SNAKING ALONG COASTS AND UP RIVERS, ENTIRE COUNTRIES TURNING RED.

PRUFROCK VOICE OVER: But they also traveled into the empty north and west....

CGI MAP SPINS AND REORIENTS, ZEROING IN ON A SINGLE ARROW DARTING OUT INTO EMPTY OCEAN, TOWARDS A LARGE ISLAND.

PRUFROCK VOICE OVER: Around 870 a man named Naddodd, who had been one of the first settlers of the Facroe Islands got lost. He ended up at a place he called 'Snowland,' what we call Iceland. Now, Iceland, during the medieval warm period was a pretty nice place, and within a century, there were 70,000 Vikings calling Iceland home.

CGI MAP SPINS AGAIN, AND REORIENTS, THE ARROW HEADS TOWARDS GREENLAND.

PRUFROCK VOICE OVER: Then, inside of a century of that, Eric the Red, who had already been exiled from Norway, got kicked out of Iceland for Murder. He sails onward to find Greenland. When his exile ends, he returns to Iceland, recruits thirty ships, and sails back to Greenland to establish Norse colonies.

A few years later, by about 986, his son, Leif Erickson, goes on from Greenland to find the coast of North America.

In a span of less than a generation, the Norse had found three unknown lands, all the way to the New World. They were the greatest explorers and seafarers before the modern era!

CGI MAP SPINS FURTHER, THE ARROWS SPLITTING AND CRAWLING ACROSS THE COASTS OF NORTH AMERICA.

PRUFROCK VOICE OVER: The Vikings sailed beyond Greenland, landing on Baffin Island, which they called Helluland, and trading with the natives. They also headed south along the Labrador coast, which they called Markland, establishing a colony on the northern tip of Newfoundland, and sailing south to the lands they called Vinland...

CUT TO: Historian Wilfred Hyde White -

WILFRED HYDE-WHITE: No one really knows for sure how far they got into North America. We were able to identify the colony at L'Anse L'Meadows in Newfoundland because the sagas describe them sailing down the east and west coast of the land - that really helps us to identify the location there. But past that... who knows. There are a lot of stories of Viking ruins and relics as far south as Maine and even New York. We're still waiting for verification. There are a lot of controversies..."

CUT TO PRUFROCK - AT THE ZOO - GRINS AT THE CAMERA.

PRUFROCK: But most importantly, what the Norse discovered were bears...

CUT TO - BIG GAY LEATHER DADDY BEAR - SMILES AND THUMBS UP.

CUT TO - URSUS HORRIBILIS, AMERICAN GRIZZLY - REARS AND ROARS AT THE CAMERA.

****

PANNING DOWN THE STACKS OF A GREAT LIBRARY, ENDLESS ROWS OF DUSTY LEATHER BOUND TOMES.

ROBIN PRUFROCK APPEARS ON CAMERA WALKS DOWN THE AISLES, FINALLY COMING TO THE AREA HE WANTS.

CAMERA FOCUSES IN ON HIM AS HE PULLS AN IMMENSE BOOK FROM THE SHELVES, BLOWS DUST OFF IT, AND OPENS THE PAGES, REVEALING COLORED MEDIEVAL ILLUSTRATIONS AND ILLUMINATED MANUSCRIPTS.

HE MAKES HIS WAY PAST THE END OF THE STACKS AND TURNS TO FACE THE CAMERA, A WHITE BACKGROUND BEHIND HIM. THE CAMERA IS CLOSE ON HIS FACE AND SHOULDERS. HE GAZES AT THE BOOK, FLIPPING PAGES.

PRUFROCK: .... No... No.... okay, here it is....

PRUFROCK LOOKS UP AT THE CAMERA AND
BEGINS TO READ

PRUFROCK READING: There are bears, too, in that region
...they differ very much from the habits of the black bears
that roam the forest... the white bear of Greenland wanders
most of the time about on the ice in the sea, hunting seals
and whales and feeding upon them. It is also as skillful a
swimmer as any seal or whale.

PRUFROCK LOOKS UP AT THE CAMERA AGAIN

PRUFROCK: The Vikings had met the Polar Bear...

CAMERA PANS BACK SLOWLY, OPENING UP FIELD
OF VIEW. THE BACKGROUND BEHIND PRUFROCK
IS REVEALED TO BE A STUFFED POLAR BEAR,
REARED UP ON ITS HIND LEGS, STANDING TEN
FEET TALL ON A PLATFORM.

QUICK CLOSE UP - PRUFROCK JERKS HIS THUMB
BACK AND GRINS AT THE CAMERA.

QUICK LONG SHOT OF PRUFROCK WITH THE
POLAR BEAR.

PRUFROCK: This guy...

CUT TO ZOO - BEARS PLAYING IN AN ENCLOSURE.
PAN TO PRUFROCK, LEANING ON THE RAILING,
WATCHING THEM. HE LOOKS UP AT THE CAMERA.

PRUFROCK: Now up to this time, the Norse had only ever
known one kind of bear. There was only one species of bear
in Europe, the brown bear.

FOCUS IN ON THE EUROPEAN BROWN BEAR,
URSUS ARCTOS, PACING IN THE ZOO ENCLOSURE.

AS THE CAMERA ZOOMS IN, THE BEAR SEEMS TO LOOK OUT AT THE AUDIENCE, AND THEN BORED, LOOKS AWAY, CONTINUING HIS PACING.

CUT TO ESTABLISHING SHOT ROBIN PRUFROCK WITH ABE WILKS, BEAR ENTHUSIAST, AND HIS PET BROWN BEAR.

CLOSE UP PRUFROCK SOMEWHAT GINGERLY, IS PETTING THE ANIMAL.

PRUFROCK: What's his name?

ABE WILKS: Tommy.

PRUFROCK: Hi Tommy.... (looks up at Wilks) Does he like to be petted?

ABE WILKS: Sure does.

PRUFROCK: So Tommy is a Brown Bear? (looks down) Are you a Brown Bear?

ABE WILKS: A European Brown Bear, that's right. Part of the family of Brown Bears, which includes the North American Grizzly Bear.

PRUFROCK: So he's a relative of the Grizzly? (to Tommy) Are you a little Grizzly? Are you? Are you? Grizzly? (to Wilks) And these were the bears that the Norsemen had in Scandinavia?

ABE WILKS: That's right.

PRUFROCK: What can you tell me about the Brown Bears.

ABE WILKS: They can get pretty big. Male European Brown Bears can run 500 to 800 pounds, five inch claws. The biggest one ever weighed more than a thousand pounds, would have stood eight feet tall upright.

PRUFROCK: That's pretty massive, how does that compare with other bears - Grizzly's or Polar Bears.

ABE WILKS: Grizzlies run about the same, but some of them can get a lot bigger. There have been Grizzly's reported up to 1500 pounds. You can tell Grizzlies by the hump.

PRUFROCK: Did the Norse ever run across Grizzly bears?

ABE WILKS: No they're mostly in the west. The Norse would never have come near them. The Norse would have met Black Bears and Polar Bears.

PRUFROCK: 1500 pounds. Is that the biggest bear ever?

ABE WILKS: No. The biggest specimens are probably the Kodiaks. Also known as Kodiak Grizzly from Alaska. Some Kodiaks have gone 1700 pounds and better. The biggest ever recorded was 2400 pounds, and there's an unverified report of one that went 3300, but I don't know about that. But those are the biggest specimens. On average, probably Polar Bears are the biggest, the males average between 700 and 1500 pounds.

PRUFROCK: Wow!

WILKS: Oh yes. The biggest polar bear ever killed weighed 2200 pounds, so the biggest Kodiak ever topped that by a little. But that Polar Bear, they figure he stood eleven feet tall. I wouldn't have liked to meet that one when he was alive.

PRUFROCK: Apart from color, how do you tell bears apart?.

ABE WILKS: Well, Polar Bears are always white. But for the rest? Oh you can't tell from color.

PRUFROCK: You can't?

ABE WILKS: Oh no. You have your black bears, your brown bears, and your polar bears. But you can have brown bears that are black. You can have black bears that are brown. Hell, I've seen a black bear that was pure white. They're all kinds of colors. I've even heard tell of blonde and red ones, though they're pretty rare.

PRUFROCK: So how do you tell the difference?

ABE WILKS: Well, how they act. For instance, brown bears can't climb trees. But black bears can. And if you lay down in front of a black bear and play dead, well, he'll just sniff you and let you alone. But if you do that with a brown bear, he'll just eat you. Some kinds, if you run, they chase. Some kinds if you shout they run.

PRUFROCK IS LAUGHING AS HE TUSSLES WITH TOMMY PLAYFULLY

PRUFROCK: So you need to know what kind of bear you're dealing with, before you decide what to do?

ABE WILKS: That's about the size of it.

PRUFROCK: So how else are they different?

ABE WILKS: Diet is a big one. Your polar bear for instance, pure meat eater. Brown bear, maybe 60% meat eater, very carnivorous, but he likes berries and greens. Black bear? a black bear is maybe 85% vegetarian, maybe more.

PRUFROCK: So my best chances are with a black bear? Throw him my salad and run for it?

ABE WILKS: You won't outrun any kind of bear, I can tell you that. They're fast enough to chase down a racehorse in a sprint. Black bears, you have to watch out, in my opinion, they're the smartest kind of bears. Their paws and wrists are different, they have more dexterity. That's how come they can climb trees while brown bears can't. I've seen black bears open jars, turn doorknobs and things like that. They're very smart, very flexible.

PRUFROCK: How big do black bears go?

WILKS: In the wild, about 200 to 600 pounds, maybe. Some of the biggest can go 900 to 1100 pounds. Those are the Labrador bears, around the north Atlantic coast. The Icelandic ones can get even bigger.

PRUFROCK: That's almost manageable size.

ABE WILKS: Ain't nothing manageable about a bear. Pound for pound, a bear is three times stronger than a gorilla. Ain't nothing stronger. I've seen bear cubs flip over a three hundred pound rock with one paw. Black Bears have killed alligators and wolverines and cougars, they've climbed up trees and stolen eggs from eagles. They go swimming for the fun of it. Grizzly Bears have killed Buffalo. Over in Asia, Brown Bears have killed Tigers.

CLOSE UP OF PRUFROCK LOOKING STARTLED.

PRUFROCK: Maybe I shouldn't be playing with Tommy here?

ABE WILKS: Might be a good idea.

****

PRUFROCK, ON A VIKING LONG SHIP, HAIR BLOWING IN THE WIND, BACK IN HIS 'HOLLYWOOD VIKING' COSTUME. OVER HIS SHOULDER, A TREE LINED COAST LOOMS.

PRUFROCK: The Norse, coming to the New World, had discovered two completely different kinds of bears from what they had known in the old country - black bears and polar bears.

Of the two, Polar bears made the biggest initial impression.

CUT TO - WILDLIFE FOOTAGE OF POLAR BEARS SWIMMING AND CLIMBING ON ICE FLOWS.

PRUFROCK VOICE OVER: Gigantic compared to the bears that they knew from home, pure white, living on ice floes and able to take to the water and swim like seals...

CUT TO - UNDERWATER, SUNLIGHT STREAMING DOWN INTO THE WATER FROM ABOVE, A SHADOW BLOCKS THE LIGHT, THEN TURBULENCE, AND A POLAR BEAR DIVES INTO THE WATER, SWIMMING UNDERWATER, IT'S MASSIVE PAWS PADDLING.

PRUFROCK: That was going to be a sensation. It was like discovering Lady Gaga.

CUT TO - CLOSE UP OF A POLAR BEAR STARING AT THE CAMERA, IT BLINKS IN SLOW MOTION.

CUT TO - ROBIN PRUFROCK, BACK IN THE LIBRARY, WITH HIS BOOK IN FRONT OF THE STUFFED POLAR BEAR.

PRUFROCK: Starting from Greenland, there was a huge export trade in polar bears: Polar bear skins, polar bear cubs if you could get them. The Norse went wild. Polar bears were one of the reasons that the Norse colonized Greenland.

PRUFROCK TURNS A PAGE IN THE BOOK, AND READS.

PRUFROCK: The first Polar Bear was brought to Europe around 900 CE as a gift to the King of Norway. In 1050, another Polar Bear was sent by the Bishop of Iceland to the Holy Roman Emperor.

CUT TO A PAINTING OF THE HOLY ROMAN
EMPEROR.

BACK TO PRUFROCK

PRUFROCK: We have laws on the books in Iceland
regulating people's pet polar bears. It was the new big thing!
If bears were a medieval Viking fashion, then polar bears
were the new black!

PRUFROCK CLOSES THE BOOK, SETS IT DOWN BY
THE POLAR BEAR.

SCENE SHIFTS TO PRUFROCK OUTDOORS,
NATURAL SUNLIGHT SHINING ON. A SAIL IS
VISIBLE BEHIND HIM. HE LOOKS OUT AT THE
SHORE, THEN GLANCES AT THE CAMERA.

PRUFROCK: Now, the other bear, the black bear, didn't
make nearly the same impression. It was smaller as bears go.
Some of them got pretty big, but by and large, they were no
bigger, and maybe a bit smaller than the hometown ones.
They were a little more timid. There didn't seem to be much
to make them stand out. And you had to travel a lot further
to get to them, to Markland. So in the normal course of
things, probably, the Norse would have just ignored them or
overlooked them. It would have been easy to do.

PRUFROCK TURNS FROM GAZING UPON THE
SHORE, DESCENDING INTO THE HOLD OF THE
LONG SHIP, WHERE HE SITS ON A BENCH. AS THE
CAMERA PANS OUT, TWO BLACK BEAR CUBS RUN
UP TO HIM. HE PUTS HIS HANDS OUT TO GREET
HIM.

PRUFROCK: Now the thing is, Iceland was a pretty happening place. Greenland was a pretty cool place. But there was one thing that these two places lacked - Good timber.

QUICK SHOT OF A MAP - ARROW POINTS TO LABRADOR COAST. LITTLE TREE ICONS APPEAR, DOTTING THE COASTLINE.

BACK TO PRUFROCK, IN THE HOLD OF THE VIKING LONGSHIP, PLAYING WITH THE BLACK BEAR CUBS.

PRUFROCK: The Norse of Greenland and Iceland were getting a lot of timber, a lot of their wood, from the old country. But that was a long way away, and after a certain point, it was just shorter and easier to go to Markland and the Labrador coast, to Newfoundland, to Vinland to get timber. We don't know how many expeditions went to Markland, it wasn't the sort of thing people kept records of back then. It was like going to the grocery store.... work, not discovery.

There are no sagas about a quick trip to Wal Mart.

But we do know about one of the first expeditions for timber, because on that expedition, something very important happened.

PRUFROCK RUBS THE HEAD OF ONE OF THE BEAR CUBS.

PRUFROCK: They encountered and killed a mother bear, and ended up with a couple of cubs, just like these cute little guys.

Sheer happenstance. Someone might have looked the other way at the wrong moment, the bear might have turned left instead of right, an arrow might have caught the wrong breeze. The bear might have got away. The Norsemen might have run away. Who knows?

But as it turned out, they killed a bear, and they had a couple of cubs....

PRUFROCK GRINS AND LOOKS UP AT THE CAMERA.

PRUFROCK: Once they had a couple of cubs, well, that was a no-brainer. Bears were big, bears were fashionable, a bear cub was worth its weight in .... whatever it is that Vikings liked. So of course they were going to bring them home, and of course they were going to end up in Iceland. That Markland expedition brought the first black bears to Iceland.

And here is how it begins.

****

CAMERA OPENS ON A SIGN 'THE WORLD FAMOUS BEAR RESTAURANT AND BARBECUE', AND BEHIND IT A LARGE CLAPBOARD BUILDING. THE CAMERA ROAMS ACROSS IT, GOING IN THROUGH THE DOOR. THE INTERIOR IS A WESTERN THEMED RESTAURANT. ROBIN PRUFROCK, SITS AT A TABLE WITH A CHECKERED BIB. BESIDE HIM STAND LUKE AND BETTY GRABLE, THE RESTAURANTS OWNERS.

PRUFROCK: You know, I still remember where I was when I learned that Teddy Roosevelt hadn't really ridden a Grizzly up San Juan hill. It was grade eight history class. Things were never the same after that. As it turns out, it's not even a Grizzly bear in the movie.

But as it turns out, Teddy did do a lot. Even if he wasn't riding a Grizzly Bear, he still charged up San Juan Hill.

He really did ride a bull moose once, at another time. I've seen pictures.

And bears? Well, he hunted his fair share, and he ate them too.

PRUFROCK LOOKS UP AT THE CAMERA, AS IF NOTICING IT FOR THE FIRST TIME.

PRUFROCK: I'm here at the World Famous Bear Rest-O-Raunt, in Wisconsin, and with me are the owners, Betty and Luke Grable, and I'm here to follow in Teddy's footsteps and sit down to a meal of Bear steak!

CAMERA FOCUSES ON BETTY AND LUKE, NODDING.

BETTY GRABLE: Hi...

LUKE GRABLE: Hello....

PRUFROCK: How long have you had this restaurant?

BETTY GRABLE: About twenty years now.

PRUFROCK: And you serve bear meat?

LUKE GRABLE: We serve a full menu.

PRUFROCK: But bear too?

BETTY GRABLE: Yes, we're first restaurant licensed in North America for bear. One of only nine today.

PRUFROCK: Is bear meat popular? What kind of bears? Do you serve grizzly?

BETTY GRABLE: We have grizzly, some polar bear, some other.

LUKE GRABLE: There's always someone that wants a grizzly bear steak, with a side order of testicles. But what you want is black bear.

BETTY GRABLE: Mostly it's black bear though.

PRUFROCK: TEASING: Panda?

BETTY GRABLE: Oh no, not Panda!

LUKE GRABLE: We get asked that. We say, they're too cute to eat.

PRUFROCK: So historically, has bear been a popular meat?

BETTY GRABLE: Well, in North America, Bear, particularly Black Bear, was a prized delicacy for the Indians. Early American settlers also ate it. In fact, at one point, it was so popular in New York, that a market was named after it.

PRUFROCK - SURPRISED AND PLEASED: Bear market? That's where the term comes from? It was an actual market for bear meat?

LUKE GRABLE: Yep. The bear market for bears, and wild meat. The bull market for cattle. That's where it's from. There you have it.

PRUFROCK: That is so cool! So, Teddy Roosevelt, he ate bear?

BETTY GRABLE: Black bear and grizzly, yes. He killed them himself.

PRUFROCK: Which did he prefer?

LUKE GRABLE: Black bear. Most people prefer black bear. Teddy said he found grizzly kind of rough.

PRUFROCK: So what is this you've prepared for me.

A WAITER PLACES A PLATE IN FRONT OF PRUFROCK AND WITHDRAWS.

BETTY GRABLE: A Black Bear steak. Piping hot. One of Teddy Roosevelt's favorite recipes.

PRUFROCK: Cool (hesitates) So, I might as well just tuck in.... (hesitates some more)

CAMERA FOCUSES ON PRUFROCK, AS HE CUTS IN WITH KNIFE AND FORK, SEIZES A PIECE, LIFTS IT TO HIS MOUTH, AND BEGINS TO CHEW THOUGHTFULLY. HE LOOKS SURPRISED. HE SWALLOWS....

PRUFROCK: Tastes like chicken!

SUBTITLE APPEARS: "Actually, it tastes like Pork! I just couldn't help myself. signed... Robin."

****

BACK TO ROBIN PRUFROCK, DRESSED UP AS A HOLLYWOOD VIKING, RIDING THE NORSE LONG BOAT INTO HARBOR. ONE OF THE BEAR CUBS IS PLAYING AT HIS FEET. HE LOOKS INTO THE CAMERA, AND THEN WAVES. THE CAMERA PANS ACROSS THE LONG BOAT, AND BACK TO PRUFROCK.

PRUFROCK: This is so cool. I'm actually sailing on an authentic Norse LONG SHIP. It's unbelievable... (To the bear cub) .... How you doing, Champ? Good?.... (Turn to audience) ... This is the city of Reykjavik on the shores of Faxafloi Bay ... (quick off camera) ... Did I say that right?

OFF SCREEN VOICE: Close enough.

PRUFROCK: And this is where those two Black Bear cubs, taken in Markland, ended up in about ten oh eight. (subtitles 1008 A.D.) The wood ended up back in Greenland, and we probably wouldn't have even heard about that, but the cubs ended up here, and we did hear about that.

PRUFROCK: So did they make a big splash? (Throws a rope out to a waiting dockhand as the LONG SHIP comes into its berth).

CUT TO - ONE OF THE CUBS CLAMBERING OVER THE SIDE, FALLING INTO THE HARBOR. SOUND OF PRUFROCK LAUGHING.

PRUFROCK VOICE OVER: Wait! Is he going to be okay? Can we help the little fellow out? (Sounds of struggle).

CUT TO - PRUFROCK HOLDING A SOAKING WET BEAR CUB, CLINGING TO HIM DESPERATELY. PRUFROCK'S HAIR IS MUSSED.

PRUFROCK: The truth is... We didn't hear much about it. Not very much. This was the Norse Bear craze after all. Everyone who was anyone had a grizzly on a leash.... (Looks off camera) Okay, not a grizzly. But a bear on a leash. Usually it was a brown bear, if you wanted to make a really big impression, a polar bear was the way to go. These little guys.... (Tussles the fur of the cub) ... there didn't seem to be anything too special about them, but there was a big market for them anyway. Any bear cub was going to fetch a good price.

CUT TO LANDSCAPE AND CITY SHOTS OF REYKJAVIK.

PRUFROCK: Now the black bears were pretty much in the shadow of polar bears. Black bears didn't make it to Europe.

They weren't nearly distinctive enough to be worth that extra leg of the trip back to the old country.

PANNING SHOT, ROBIN PRUFROCK AND TOM HAGGERTY, ANTHROPOLOGIST, WALKING THROUGH A PARK IN REYKJAVIK. THEY ARE BOTH HOLDING BLACK BEAR CUBS. THE SWEDISH BIKINI TEAM ROLLS PAST.

IN THE BACKGROUND, THE BIG GAY BEAR IS BUYING A HOT DOG FROM A STREET VENDOR, HE WAVES AT THE CAMERA.

PRUFROCK: But American Black Bears caught on in Iceland. How come?

TOM HAGGERTY: (looking dubiously at the small bear on a harness and leash) He's not going to bite me? Is he?

PRUFROCK: Oh no, they're sweethearts!

HAGGERTY'S BEAR ROLLS OVER ON ITS SIDE, AND PLAYFULLY WRAPS ITS PAWS AROUND HAGGERTY'S FOOT.

TOM HAGGERTY: I'm pretty sure he's biting me. Nibbling me anyway.

PRUFROCK: He's licking you. He likes you. Anyway...

TOM HAGGERTY: Right. Iceland. Well, there were several things going on. One was convenience. Given the distances, it was as feasible to bring black bears from Greenland and Markland, as it was to bring brown bears from Norway.

PRUFROCK: Everyone wanted a bear of their own!

TOM HAGGERTY: That's overstating it a little. Bears were never what you would call common. Not like cats or dogs. They were an exotic status pet, like owning a lion or a jaguar.

And to be frank, the supply had never been great, which cemented their status as an exotic pet. But that made them valuable and valued.

Especially for Iceland, which didn't actually have any native mammals, apart from seals and the occasional polar bear or arctic fox. So actually having a large animal, or even a large wild animal hide, that had an unusual cachet. More than it did in Norway, which had more access to wildlife and furs.

In fact, the economics favored black bears. Greenland was a pretty marginal place. Markland was even further out, unoccupied by the Norse, and mainly they just went there for the wood. It was a pretty tough living out in the Greenland colony. So, for the Greenlanders, bringing back a couple of cubs, or some bear skins, well, that didn't take up a lot of space in their boats. Not compared to wood. But it could make a huge difference to the success of the expedition.

So they were bringing them back steadily. And along with bear cubs and bear hides... or sometimes instead of, they could also bring back beaver and caribou hide. Some speculate that the Newfoundland colony would not have survived nearly as long as it did without the extra stimulus of the bear trade and its spin offs.

CUTAWAY - CGI GRAPHIC LABRADOR TO ICELAND - ARROW MOVING FROM NEWFOUNDLAND. 8 BIT BEAR GRAPHIC.

PRUFROCK VOICE OVER: By 1100 as many as a hundred American black bear cubs had found their way to Iceland.

CUT BACK TO PRUFROCK AND HAGGERTY. THEY'RE WALKING ALONG NOW. HAGGERTY'S BEAR IS MORE PLAYFUL, HE'S PULLING ON HIS LEASH.

The Bear Cavalry – Page 32

PRUFROCK: Was that the only thing.

TOM HAGGERTY: Not quite. Brown bears got unmanageable very quickly, and no matter how much status you craved it wasn't worth losing an arm. Black bears proved more versatile. They had more dexterity, they could be taught more tricks. The perception that seemed to emerge was that they were much more manageable and easier to deal with than brown bears. The Icelanders started calling them 'Gentle Bears. So black bears were inherently more popular.

If it had just been brown bears, I think the bear fad would have faded much more quickly. Much more costly, much less reliable. Those were the perceptions.

PRUFROCK: Was that just the perception? Or was there something to it?

TOM HAGGERTY - (CHUCKLES): Well, they were bears. But black bears were probably smaller, and that may have contributed to it. Smaller bears, easier to handle…

PRUFROCK: I know a guy who would argue with that.

THEY COME TO A PARK BENCH, AND SIT DOWN. HAGGERTY SHOWS VISIBLE RELIEF WHEN HE PUTS DOWN HIS CUB AND IT SCAMPERS OVER TO PLAY WITH ROBIN'S CUB.

TOM HAGGERTY: Well, yes. And of course, there was diet.

PRUFROCK: Diet?

TOM HAGGERTY: American black bears habitually consume a lot more vegetation and insects than European brown bears. That made them dramatically easier and cheaper to feed. And safer. That was probably a good thing for many Icelanders.

PRUFROCK: Probably a psychological factor as well? We're made of meat ourselves, so the more of a meat eater we've got, the more we have to worry about our being on the menu.

TOM HAGGERTY: Quite. I never thought of that. I suppose one slept slightly easier with a black bear, than a brown bear in the household. Actually, the brown bears did suffer in the comparison, they came to be perceived as quite a nuisance, and the Icelanders actually passed laws forbidding the importation of brown bears eventually.

CUT TO ILLUMINATED MANUSCRIPT. AS THE CAMERA SCROLLS DOWN, A VOICE OVER IS READ OUT IN AN ICELANDIC ACCENT.

VOICE OVER: "Laws of Early Iceland - The penalty is also outlawry if men ship a Brown Bear out here to Iceland. The bears owner and the ships master incur that penalty, but members of the ships company a fine of three marks. Nine neighbors are to be called at assembly for all lesser outlawry cases, and five for a fine. If a Brown Bear gets loose here in Iceland and does damage to people or to men's stock, then the man who brought the bear out here takes full responsibility for it in the same way as for any other tame bear."

PRUFROCK: So they actually passed a law forbidding brown bears specifically?

TOM HAGGERTY: Brown bears, yes.

PRUFROCK: What about polar bears or black bears?

TOM HAGGERTY: They were subject to Icelandic law too, but there was no prohibition on import. In the case of Polar Bears, I think that was because of European trade, Polar

Bears were very valuable. Black Bears.... I guess they had the reputation of being more manageable.

PRUFROCK: So that was it for Brown Bears?

TOM HAGGERTY: Oh yes. You see, bears weren't breeding in Iceland back then. Being around bears, even tame ones in mating season is a really bad idea generally, and being around mother bears and cubs was an even worse one. So most of the tame bears in Iceland were tamed as cubs or brought over. If you forbid importing brown bears, eventually no more brown bears. It's just the polar bears and the black bears.

PRUFROCK: There was one more reason, I've heard, that had people preferring black bears to brown ones.

HAGGERTY (BLANK FOR A SECOND, THEN RESPONDING TO PRUFROCK'S PROMPT): Oh yes, the reputation was that black bears tasted better.

CLOSE UP OF PRUFROCK, GRINNING INTO CAMERA: Tastes like chicken!

SUBTITLE: "PORK! Sorry again. Robin"

****

MONTAGE OF VIKING RAIDS, STOCK FOOTAGE.

CUT TO, BIG GAY BEAR IN THONG AND VIKING HELMET, HOLDING A RUBBER SWORD. HE IS GRINNING. AS HE GRINS, THE SWORD WOBBLES AND THEN DROOPS. ONE OF THE HORNS FALLS OFF HIS HELMET. CLOSE UP ON FACE, HE LOOKS WORRIED.

CUT TO - ROBIN PRUFROCK AND HISTORIAN, WILFRED HYDE WHITE IN A HIGH END RESTAURANT.

PRUFROCK: What is this?

WILFRED HYDE WHITE: This is a classic Scandinavian dish, quite exquisite.

ROBIN: Bear?

WILFRED HYDE WHITE GIVES ROBIN A LONG BLANK STARE, LIP CURLS SLIGHTLY. FINALLY...

WILFRED HYDE WHITE: .....no.

PRUFROCK: All right, so its about 1150 A.D., what's happening?

WILFRED HYDE WHITE: The Viking Era is coming to an end.

PRUFROCK: And this is coinciding with the end of the Medieval warm period, so it's not as warm in Scandinavia, growing seasons are shorter, there's less food production, population declines, especially in comparison to the south.

WILFRED HYDE-WHITE GIVING ANOTHER BLANK STARE - A SHORT PAUSE

WILFRED HYDE-WHITE: Well, that's certainly a fashionable, climate based interpretation, and there's undoubtedly something to it. But you have to remember, by this time, the Norse had been raiding Europe for something like three hundred years.

PRUFROCK: People were getting tired of it?

WILFRED HYDE WHITE: Indeed. As you so eloquently put it, 'People' were getting tired of it. And they were learning to cope. You had changes in military tactics, they were learning to fight off the invaders. You had changes in metallurgy, better weapons, in fortifications. Social organization.... States were becoming more advanced and sophisticated, better communication, larger armies. Southern Europeans are sailing themselves, their ships are getting bigger and better.

Gunpowder and firearms are about to make an appearance in the next few centuries. In many of these areas, Norse colonies had formed and assimilated with the local population. They didn't appreciate being raided by their relatives, and were willing to help fight back. In England you had the Norman Conquest in 1066, and after that, England is a very different place, not nearly such easy pickings...

PRUFROCK: So as far as the Norse were concerned, the free ride was over?

WILFRED HYDE-WHITE - BLANK STARE: Yes.... That's a succinct way to put it. 'The free ride is over.'

CAMERA PANS ACROSS THE RESTAURANT, CLOSES IN ON THE BIG GAY BEAR, NOW WITH ONLY ONE HORN ON HIS HELMET, DROWNING HIS SORROWS IN A PLATE OF SPAGHETTI.

****

CAMERA OPENS ON AN EMPTY FIELD. PANS AND ZOOMS IN ON A CORNER OF THE FIELD. ROBIN PRUFROCK SITS ON A BUCKET, VIKING WEAPONS AND ARMOUR AT HIS FEET. HE IS WEARING A BLANKET OVER HIS SHOULDERS. AS THE CAMERA APPROACHES, HE LOOKS UP.

The Bear Cavalry — Page 37

PRUFROCK: It's 1250. The age of Viking raids is over. The fury of the Norsemen has passed. The medieval warm period is over. The world is changing...

The medieval glacial period is starting up. Viking power in Europe is in decline. The centers are shifting south to the areas of population and civilization. The Norse are in decline.

CUT TO CGI MAP OF THE NORTH ATLANTIC. A MIXTURE OF GREENS AND BLUES AND GRAYS AND WHITES. THE GRAY AND THE WHITE IS CREEPING SOUTH. SNOWFLAKES FALL OVER THE MAP. POPULATION BAR GRAPHS APPEAR BESIDE VARIOUS SCANDINAVIAN COUNTRIES, DROPPING INTO RED.

PRUFROCK VOICE OVER: Population is dropping. Crop yields are dropping. Grain is getting harder to raise. It won't grow any more in northern Norway. It's not growing any more in Greenland. It's getting harder to sail the northern seas, the sea ice comes further south. Vinland is abandoned. Contact is lost with Greenland.

THOSE PARTS OF THE MAP GROW DARK.

Iceland is hanging on. But barley is in decline, and it's eventually going to fail. Crops are going to shift towards ground crops - carrots and parsnips, radishes, onions. Cattle will decline, sheep will take their place. There's going to be a lot more fish in people's diets.

Hard times are coming.

CUT TO PRUFROCK, SITTING IN THE CORNER OF THE FIELD, HUDDLING UNDER HIS BLANKET.

So where do bears fit in all this?

CAMERA CUTS TO BIG GAY BEAR: Hey Robin?

CUT TO PRUFROCK, LOOKING UP. CAMERA ZOOMS OUT. ROBIN PRUFROCK, SITTING ON BUCKET IN FIELD, BLANKET OVER HIS SHOULDERS, LOOKS UP. BIG GAY BEAR IN THONG AND ONE-HORNED VIKING HELMET IS STANDING NEXT TO HIM.

PRUFROCK: Yeah?

BIG GAY BEAR: Are you ready? Crew wants to wrap up and get to the next scene before it rains.

PRUFROCK: Oh right, yes sure. (Turns to camera) ... Oh by the way, everyone, this is Paul Bjornson, he's on our crew.

PAUL BJORNSON: Sound mix editor.

PRUFROCK: I just wanted to introduce him, because we've been using him a lot.

PAUL BJORNSON: I'm not actually gay.

PRUFROCK: But he is 6'6", incredibly hairy and of Scandinavian descent. So his direct ancestors probably pillaged Europe.

PAUL BJORNSON: Not that my ancestors are admitting to anything.

PRUFROCK: Plausible deniability.

PAUL BJORNSON: When we were brainstorming this documentary, we were kicking a lot of ideas around. Basically, we're doing this series on really strange corners of human culture, Bear Cavalry, Odd civilizations, and the hyper-masculine iconography of Vikings and bear riding really just seemed to mesh with the hyper-masculine archetype of the 'bear' in modern gay culture, so it seemed like fun to play them off against each other.

PRUFROCK: You can tell who has the Master's Degree in Deep Literary Theory.

THE TWO MEN STAND UP AND WALK OFF TOGETHER, BACKS TO THE CAMERA.

PAUL BJORNSON VOICE OVER: Yeah, but try and find a job in that field.

PRUFROCK VOICE OVER: It seemed like a fun thing, I mean, this is a very weird area of culture, and there's a lot of dry history to it, so it seemed like a good idea to jazz it up - merging archaic hyper-masculine references with modern ones.

PAUL BJORNSON VOICE OVER: Not a new idea, the Village People were there first.

PRUFOCK VOICE OVER: Anyway, we auditioned a lot of gay men. But Paul was bigger than any of them. So we ended up putting him in front of the camera.

PAUL BJORNSON VOICE OVER: I get to keep the costumes though. My wife likes the thong. I have to mention though, one of the horns fell off my helmet.

PRUFROCK VOICE OVER: Really? We'll have to fix that. Talk to props. It turns out, Viking helmets didn't even have horns.

PAUL BJORNSON VOICE OVER: The comic books lied to us. Who would have thought? You know, some people think your mustache makes you look gay. That handlebar thing you've got going on. That or a hipster. Not that there's anything wrong with being gay. Hipster on the other hand…

PRUFROCK VOICE OVER: Hmm. My son thinks it makes me look like a fireman. He's always drawing me with an axe.

PAUL BJORNSON VOICE OVER: Maybe he thinks it makes you look like a serial killer?

PRUFROCK VOICE OVER: No, he draws me with the hat too.

PAUL BJORNSON VOICE OVER: Oh, well, definitely fireman. I think all kids would like their dads to be like that. Firemen or cops, heroes and stuff like that.

PRUFROCK VOICE OVER: It's hard to explain what I do to him. Documentary film making... It's sort of abstract. So... what are we shooting next? Am I talking about eating bear again?

PAUL BJORNSON VOICE OVER: You've got a lot of that in there.

PRUFROCK VOICE OVER: You don't think it's gay to be talking about eating bear, is it? Not that there's anything wrong with that.

THEY ARE ALMOST OUT OF CAMERA SIGHT.

PAUL BJORNSON VOICE OVER: Being gay? Or eating bear?

PRUFROCK VOICE OVER: Well...

PAUL BJORNSON VOICE OVER: Just messing with you. I don't think that there's any sexual assignment to eating bear one way or another. No cultural baggage to it. Now, if it was bull testicles? That's tied up with cultural baggage.

PRUFROCK VOICE OVER: Hey, did you know Teddy Roosevelt didn't actually ride a grizzly bear up San Juan Hill? It was just a regular horse.

PAUL BJORNSON VOICE OVER: You're kidding!

The Bear Cavalry – Page 41

PRUFROCK: No, it was just the movie. It wasn't even a real Grizzly Bear in the movie.

PAUL BJORNSON VOICE OVER: Well now I feel like my childhood just got raped!

FADE TO BLACK AND TRANSITION...

****

OPEN ON A STREET SCENE IN REYKJAVIK, PEOPLE WALKING BACK AND FORTH. A MAN WALKS A BEAR ON A LEASH, THEY STOP AT A STREETLIGHT AND WAIT BEFORE CROSSING. THE CAMERA PANS OUT TO ROBIN PRUFROCK AND TOM HAGGERTY HAVING A BEER IN A SIDEWALK CAFÉ.

PRUFROCK: So what happened with this fad of keeping bears as pets? Did it die out? When did it die out?

TOM HAGGERTY: It's not something that people kept elaborate records on, so we don't really know. Maybe twelfth or thirteenth centuries. European brown bears were big, dangerous, volatile animals. In a sense, it never really died out.

The Shakespearean English had their bear gardens, where bears were used for blood sports. Bear baiting was a popular sport in England until the 19th century.

As late as the 18th century, Lord Byron, the Romantic Poet, when he was a student in England, he kept a tame bear as a pet. It was some sort of poetic statement. I don't think he stuck with it. So it kept on.

There was always someone who was going to want an exotic pet. People still do that today, but its Mike Tyson with a Tiger, or Pablo Escobar with his hippos.

Bears remained a big part of popular culture.

PRUFROCK: In Circuses and Zoos, constantly. In seventies television....

QUICK CUT TO: GRIZZLY ADAMS, TV SERIES CLIP.

BACK TO PRUFROCK AND HAGGERTY IN THE TAVERN.

TOM HAGGERTY: The Viking Age was over, and the Little Ice Age was kicking in. But it's not fair to say that Scandinavian culture was in decline. I mean, their technology was getting better, literature, art, farming. The Kalmar Union was coming up. There were Swedish and Danish Empires. But I think it is fair to say that Scandinavia from say the 13th or 14th century on was basically being absorbed into the larger European mainstream.

But the whole set of archaic traditions, the custom of bears as pets for the great and powerful, that was in steep decline after the 13th century. There were contributing factors - Greenland had fallen out of contact, that was the main source for polar bears, so that exotic was no longer available, and the kind of push they'd given to the fashion was no longer there.

PRUFROCK: Except in Iceland?

HAGGERTY (NODDING): Except in Iceland.

PAN OUT TO THE STREET SCENE. AT THE CORNER, RETURNING, THE BEAR ON THE LEASH STAND UP ON HIS HIND LEGS TO LOOK AROUND.

****

ON A HILL LOOKING DOWN OVER A STRANGE COMPLEX OF LOG BUILDINGS AND CHAIN LINK FENCES. AS THE CAMERA SWEEPS, WE SEE

The Bear Cavalry — Page 43

SEVERAL BLACK BEARS ROAMING THE GROUNDS. ROBIN PRUFROCK SITS ON A FOLDING LAWN CHAIR, WITH BINOCULARS, AND A THERMOS OF COFFEE.

THE MORNING IS COLD, YOU CAN SEE HIS BREATH. THE CAMERA APPROACHES. HE LOOKS AT IT.

PRUFROCK: This is Astrunggottir, an Icelandic Bear farm. This is not one of those factory farms that you hear about, where bear gall bladders and bear bile is harvested for the Asian market.

The Icelanders are not into factory farming. Especially not with bears. These are free range bears. As free range as possible...

CAMERA SWIVELS FROM PRUFROCK, ACROSS THE FARM. ON THE SLOPE BELOW, A MAN IS CLIMBING TOWARDS PRUFROCK. BACK TO PRUFROCK, WATCHING THE MAN COME UP THE HILL.

PRUFROCK: (muttering under his breath) I'd like to see trying to cage up bears like they do in a chicken farm.... (Louder) That's Halvi Ingolfs the owner of the farm coming towards us. He's going to show us around the farm.

HALVI ARRIVES, HE AND PRUFROCK SHAKE HANDS, HEAD TOWARDS THE FARM.

CUT TO - A BEAR LICKING HALVI INGOLFS HAND, AS HE FEEDS IT.

PRUFROCK: I don't know that I'd want to do that. We actually ran a lot of this stuff by our insurers, and this is where they drew the line. NO HAND FEEDING THE BEARS. That was in black and white.

THE CAMERA SWIVELS AWAY FROM PRUFROCK
AND HALVI INGOLFS, BRIEFLY SHOWING SOME
OF THE FILM CREW. IN THE GROUP, A MAN IN A
BLACK SUIT STANDS, WITHOUT A SPECIFIC
PURPOSE. A SUBTITLE APPEARS "The Insurance Guy."
THE CAMERA RETURNS TO PRUFROCK AND
HALVI INGOLFS.

HALVI INGOLFS: You can, you know. Try. (His accent is
almost impenetrably thick, and it is apparent that English is
not his language.)

PRUFROCK: We actually have a guy from the insurance
company on the crew to make sure I don't do anything stupid
like that.

QUICK SHOT TO THE MAN IN A SUIT, STANDING
WITH THE CAMERA CREW. HE WAVES.

HALVI LAUGHS.

PRUFROCK: I'd like to talk about the history a bit. You are
breeding bears here...

HALVI INGOLFS: Yah....

PRUFROCK: Okay, as I understand it - in the old days, what
people would do is that they would just take cubs from the
wild, and raise the cubs up tame.

HALVI INGOLFS: Yah....

PRUFROCK: There were good reasons for that. No matter
how tame, mating season was going to be incredibly
dangerous....

HALVI INGOLFS - (CHUCKLES): Yah, they are a handful,
for sure...

PRUFROCK: To say nothing of what a mother bear is like when she has cubs.

QUICK CUT TO URSUS HORRIBILIS ROARING.

CUT TO PRUFROCK - AT THE CAMERA.

PRUFROCK: I'm sorry, Halvi's got a bit too much trouble with the English language, it's not working out well. We're going to try something else.

CUT TO: ROBIN PRUFROCK AND TOM HAGGERTY OUTSIDE THE BEAR FARM, LOOKING AT BEARS PLAY FROM THE OTHER SIDE OF A CHAIN LINK FENCE.

PRUFROCK: So around the thirteenth century, the Icelanders are still keeping bears.... And they're breeding them. What's going on? How does this happen?

TOM HAGGERTY: You have to realize how it all hangs together. Iceland was essentially a colonial society. Colonial societies put a lot of time and energy into reproducing the homeland, or their memory of the homeland. So the Icelanders were a lot more committed to the old Norse traditions, the old Norse ways of life, than the homeland actually was.

PRUFROCK: So Norway and Norwegians could move along, because they were Norwegians. They were comfortable with who they were, so they could take the next step. But the Icelanders, they were trying to be Norwegians, or what they remembered Norway being. So they couldn't move, they were stuck there....

TOM HAGGERTY: Precisely.

PRUFROCK: And so they were preserving the old language, the old habits, the old customs.... One of which was lords and nobles keeping bears for pets as a status symbol.

TOM HAGGERTY: Correct.

PRUFROCK: How does that get them to breeding their own?

TOM HAGGERTY: Simple. They were running out of bears.

PRUFROCK LAUGHS OUT LOUD

TOM HAGGERTY: They had passed laws forbidding the importation of brown bears from Europe. They were just too dangerous, too uncontrollable.

So that left polar bears from Greenland, and black bears from Markland. But as Greenland slowly falls out of contact with Iceland, those sources are drying up. Which means that there's a lot of cultural demand, and fewer and fewer bears to go around. They're getting more and more valuable. Economics.

PRUFROCK: So at some point, someone decides to put bear and bear together and start making their own.

TOM HAGGERTY: Precisely.

PRUFROCK: When does this take place?

TOM HAGGERTY: We're not sure. The first instances are probably unrecorded. It may have happened way back. But we do know that after a while, it becomes a real thing. Bear breeding becomes a hobby of the upper classes, or whatever passes for an upper class in Iceland, and there's a lot of correspondence, a lot of negotiation, a lot of examination of bloodlines, contracts over who gets the cubs. Eventually, whose bear is doing what to whom becomes a matter of high politics, it's a serious matter, it reflects arrangements, seals alliances. Who gets a cub and when is reflecting the social dynamics. Bears are the currency of the aristocracy, they're the flow of relationships.

If you look at the correspondence of the fourteenth century, it's amazing. It's all bears, bears, bears. But really, if you dig a little deeper, it's really about how the nobility are relating to each other. Who is in, who is out, who is ascending. It's about exchanging favors, making alliances, cementing marriages. Fascinating stuff. It's all about bears on the surface, but beneath the surface, it's about everything else.

PRUFROCK: Why didn't this happen before? Why wasn't this happening in Scandinavia?

TOM HAGGERTY: I think they sort of tried. You have all kinds of records of polar bears being given to the King of Denmark, or the Holy Roman Emperor. The Tsar gets a bear. The king of France gives a bear. ..... But it was the wrong kind of bear.

PRUFROCK: The wrong kind?

TOM HAGGERTY: European brown bears.

CUT TO CLIP OF GRIZZLY ROARING. TEETH AND CLAWS.

TOM HAGGERTY: They were large, they could get unpredictable especially in breeding, or with cubs. They were primarily carnivorous. The meat wasn't all that valuable. There were cumulative downsides.

PRUFROCK: So the black bears weren't as dangerous to breed?

CUT TO FRIENDLY LOOKING BLACK BEARS GAMBOLLING AT HALVI INGOLFS FARM, HAPPY MUSIC. FRIENDLY VIBE.

TOM HAGGERTY: Oh no They were just as dangerous They're giant, awesomely strong predators with huge claws and teeth. It's just not safe.

CUT TO FRIENDLY NATURE CLIP OF BLACK BEARS, WITH A BIG RED X ON THEM.

TOM HAGGERTY: But the thing was, breeding cattle, bulls aren't safe either. There's a lot of risk with any of the big domesticates. The real question isn't whether it's safe, but how badly do you want it? How motivated are you?

PRUFROCK: So in Scandinavia, the motivation isn't there. But the Icelanders, they were highly motivated. They were clinging to the old ways, and those included having a bear to show your status.

TOM HAGGERTY: The Icelanders were very motivated. Definitely. And they were lucky in that they had a very good bear to work with. They had enough advantages - they were smaller, they were more manageable normally, they had better fur, they had much better meat, their diets were mostly vegetarian so they could be fed more cheaply. They had enough advantages, they had enough things going for them that people wanted to take the chance, to take the risk.

PRUFROCK: So Black Bears you could do it? And brown bears you couldn't?

TOM HAGGERTY: Well, by that time all they had was black bears to work with. But it was a matter of cumulative proportions, not really an off and on. You could breed brown bears, if you really wanted to put the time and effort and risk in. But was it worth it? 50/50. You'd add up all the advantages and disadvantages you had with brown bears and it would be 30 or 35 .... Not worth it. Or you could stick with pigs, but that was a lot of work, it was expensive and difficult keeping them alive in that climate. 40 or 45. You'd add up all the advantages and disadvantages of black bears, and it would be 51 or 55, not too much different, but just enough to make it worth doing.

PRUFROCK: So what was the key, what made the difference....

TOM HAGGERTY MAKES A FACE

TOM HAGGERTY: It's really hard to pin it down.

SUBTITLES APPEAR - "I know the feeling, it was really hard to pin Tom down. Signed Robin"

TOM HAGGERTY: It's a combination of thing.... But meat. Bear meat.

QUICK CUT TO PAUL BJORNSON, TRYING TO GLUE A HORN BACK ON HIS HELMET. - LOOKS UP AT THE CAMERA.

PAUL BJORNSON: He's a bit obsessed with bear meat....

****

ROBIN PRUFROCK, IN A CLASSROOM WITH A DUNCE CAP, AND PROFESSOR'S ROBES.

PRUFROCK: All right, time for a quick lesson in food economics.

TAKES OFF THE DUNCE CAP.

PRUFROCK: I like a good steak. But a steak isn't free. I'm not talking dollars and cents here. For every pound of meat, an animal represents maybe fifty pounds of vegetation consumed. Grain fed beef is very expensive, because it means that for every pound of steak we eat, we're giving up fifty pounds of grain you could feed people with. If grain is cheap enough, if beef is expensive enough, it makes sense.

If on the other hand, your beef is grass fed, then people can't eat grass. That makes a lot more sense. Of course, if you are raising grass where you could have raised wheat, it makes less sense.

This is what food economics comes down to. Choices, inputs, outputs, return on investment.

ROBIN PRUFROCK WALKS CASUALLY ACROSS THE CLASSROOM. THE WALL ENDS. THE CAMERA PULLS BACK TO REVEAL THAT THE CLASSROOM IS A MOCK UP - TWO WALLS AND SOME FLOOR AND DESK. THE CLASSROOM 'SET' IS IN THE MIDDLE OF A FARMYARD. THERE ARE COWS, CHICKENS AND SHEEP ROAMING AROUND, AND IN THE MIDDLE, A TIGER. PRUFROCK WALKS UP TO THE TIGER AND PETS IT.

PRUFROCK: We don't eat tiger steaks because tigers eat meat, meat is expensive to produce. So a steak from a tiger is a lot more expensive, maybe fifty times or a hundred times more expensive than a steak from a cow. One is just so much more expensive to feed.

Now, we're basically a grain based society - wheat, rice, barley, millet, rapeseed, canola, corn... Grains are basically grasses. It's no coincidence that most of our domesticated animals, horses and cattle, camels, goats, sheep are all grazers, grass eaters. For most of our history, our meat has been free, or at least pretty low cost, because we've been raising them on the by-products of things that we eat.

In fact almost all of our domesticates, chickens, guinea pigs, pigs, dogs... they're all eating things that we don't eat, so the meat is in a sense, free. Sometimes they eat our leftovers, but the thing is that they're all relatively cheap to feed.

I mentioned grain fed beef, that goes against the grain so to speak. That's a modern deviation, but this is how it works.

PRUFROCK LOOKS OFF THE CAMERA, TOWARD AN UNSEEN DIRECTOR.

PRUFROCK: Are we good?

OFF CAMERA MUMBLING.

PRUFROCK: Okay, let's go back to Vikings.

CUT TO THE FJORDS. AERIAL VIEW OF THE ICELANDIC LANDSCAPE. PRUFROCK AND TOM HAGGERTY IN THE AIRPLANE, LOOKING OUT OVER THE COUNTRYSIDE.

TOM HAGGERTY: The Norse people had the same diets, they ate pretty much everything that we did. Not potatoes or corn, that hadn't come over from the New World yet. But pretty much the rest of it. They grew a lot of barley, that's what they used to make their beer. The Vikings loved beer.

PRUFROCK: Don't we all?

PRUFROCK RAISES A TALL BEER MUG.

TOM HAGGERTY: Where did you get that? Anyway, they raised cattle, sheep, goats and pigs. Cattle, particularly, were vital to the Norse. They lived in a northern territory, growing seasons were short. It was actually too far north for cattle, so they invested a lot of time and effort into building immense barns and cultivating and storing hay. They lived on milk and meat.

PRUFROCK (ADDRESSING THE CAMERA): Cattle were also a major source of draft labor - for plowing fields, for carrying packs, for wagons. There was a lot of horsepower there, and they made use of it. It was pretty essential.

TOM HAGGERTY: Cattle, of course, along with horses, sheep and goats were all grassland browsers.

PRUFROCK: All except pigs....

TOM HAGGERTY: Pigs are the odd man out. They're much more omnivores, they eat scraps, roughage. Pigs were something of a luxury food, because they were more expensive to feed and keep, particularly the farther north you went, because they didn't adapt well to cold temperatures. They were farmed extensively in Denmark. But they were also in Norway and Sweden, and even in Iceland.

PRUFROCK: That's the standard package in Scandinavia: Cattle, horses, sheep, goats and pigs. So what starts to happen in Iceland?

TOM HAGGERTY: Well, we're getting into the medieval glacial now, and it's getting colder. Shorter growing seasons. Crops are down. There's less and less barley. Even grasslands for hay are less productive, it's getting too expensive for cows. So for a lot of people, they're shifting to smaller, cheaper animals, sheep and goats. They still get milk, they still get leather, they get wool and meat.

PRUFROCK: NODS

TOM HAGGERTY: Now at this time there are pigs in Iceland. The Norse brought them over along with everything else. But they're in decline, because the climate is getting worse and worse.

PRUFROCK: They're expensive to keep.

TOM HAGGERTY: Oddly, that's a yes and no kind of thing. Remember that grasslands, hayfields and barley fields are declining. But a lot of the root crops, the leafies, the things that pigs eat, that's holding up better. That's not declining as fast. So comparatively, the economics are shifting a bit. Food is getting more costly to produce right across the board, and cattle and barley are getting very expensive. The cost of feeding pigs aren't getting as expensive as fast.

PRUFROCK (A LITTLE CONFUSED): So, in a sense, they're getting cheaper?

TOM HAGGERTY: In a sense. It's getting more expensive to feed them, but the expenses aren't rising as fast. The trouble is that there's another expense in keeping them. They are getting harder to maintain as the weather gets colder and colder. They're not as winter tolerant. So you have to put more work in for them. So the economics start to work somewhat for them one way, works hard against them another way, and they're basically in serious decline in Iceland. Pigs are a luxury, its high status, reserved for the nobility or for special occasions. What Iceland needs is cold tolerant pigs, or a cold tolerant animal that is an effective substitute, in terms of diet and meat.

PRUFROCK: And this is where bears come in....

TOM HAGGERTY: American Black Bears yes. What's distinctive about American Black Bears, what distinguishes them from say the Brown Bears is their diet. They eat a lot of plant material, 85% of their diet, they eat insects, fish, meat is a pretty small proportion of their diet. They're good scavengers. They'll take the leftovers, the scraps, the garbage..

PRUFROCK: That sounds like a diet very close to pigs...

TOM HAGGERTY: Very much like pigs. Very similar. But the black bears are much more cold tolerant than pigs... They've got their own ways of coping with winter.

PRUFROCK (INTERRUPTING): I have a confession.

HAGGERTY - LOOKING EXPECTANT

PRUFROCK: I keep saying that bear tastes just like chicken.... But actually, it's a lot more like pork.

TOM HAGGERTY (NODDING): The tastes are very similar. The Icelandic Norse had several names for the black bear - 'Black Bear' of course. 'Clever Bear' because they were known to climb, to swim, to open jars and doors. 'Gentle Bear' because they thought they were easier to handle. 'Pig Bear' for the taste of the meat. And in fact, in the fourteenth century, as the animals numbers grew, they started to be raised extensively as a meat animal.

PRUFROCK: They replaced pigs.

TOM HAGGERTY: Pigs did vanish from Iceland. But it's a little bit more complicated than that. It was coming from two separate directions. On the one hand, you had that whole Norse culture revolving around bears, you had all that historical social baggage going all the way back to berserkers, and raising cubs as pets, and the development of a local managed population of black bears being established as a sort of status symbol.

And then, you had a bear species that was very fluid and adaptable to that culture, and so there was a lot of incentive to move up to the next level there. And on the other hand, you had a high status meat animal, pigs, which were really having coping issues, and you had an animal which was already high status, very similar meat, similar diet, which was able to step into that niche.

Pork was becoming a status specialty food as it got rarer and rarer, and more and more expensive. But Bear tasted very similar, so it acquired the same cachet. It moved from simply a weird exotic pet, to something that actually had use.

PRUFROCK: So the end result was that bears became a domesticated species in Iceland...

TOM HAGGERTY: They proliferated, yes. They transitioned from something that was the province of the nobility, from a marker of status, and spread through Icelandic society. Meat and fur, leather... Eventually labor, yes. It was a unique event.

CUT BACK TO PRUFROCK IN BLACK PROFESSORS ROBES IN THE FARMER'S FIELD, HE MOVES BACK INTO THE CLASSROOM, PICKS UP A CHICKEN OFF A SCHOOL DESK AND SHOES IT ALONG. HE FACES THE CAMERA.

PRUFROCK: Because normally, the economics for bear domestication just don't work. It's always cheaper to raise cattle or horses, or pigs. The Norse never domesticated bears before, because they'd always had better domesticates, and their only available bear was a relatively poor chose.

Economics isn't black and white, it's all about variables shifting, and in Iceland, in the 13th and 14th centuries, climate change, the little ice age was making those variables shift around. They shifted to a place where it made sense to domesticate bears, where it was economic, and it had never been economic before.

The Bear Cavalry – Page 56

CUT BACK TO PRUFROCK AND HAGGERTY ON THE AIRPLANE.

TOM HAGGERTY: Correct. The key was that a population of bears was available in Iceland to exploit in this new way. This wouldn't have worked with the brown bear. But now, you had a particular place, where they had a better kind of bear, where they had a culture which was for its own reasons needing to make that social investment to hang on to a particular tradition, you had a situation where the traditional domesticates were in relative decline, where the production was favoring this animal, and where there was a less effective domesticate in a very similar role that they could displace.

PRUFROCK: So the end result was that Bears became a domesticated species in Iceland...

TOM HAGGERTY: Yes.

PRUFROCK: I said that.

TOM HAGGERTY: But I said it smarter.

PRUFROCK (GRINS): Touché.

****

MONTAGE OPENING SHOT, THE HALVI FARM, PANNING THROUGH THE FARM, FARMER AT WORK, THE BEARS OUTSIDE IN THE FIELDS, FEEDING FROM PENS. MONTAGE OF NORSE BEAR IMAGERY, SCULPTURES AND WOODCUTS. SHOTS OF PAUL THE BIG GAY BEAR, SHOTS OF THE RESTAURANT, WITH LUKE AND BETTY.

PRUFROCK VOICE OVER: In Iceland, in the thirteenth and fourteenth century, something had happened that hadn't happened in the old world for thousands of years. The

Icelanders had domesticated a major new animal - the American Black Bear.

THE MONTAGE GIVES WAY TO SCENES OF A FAIR, CHILDREN WALKING BY WITH BEAR SHAPED HELIUM BALLOONS, VENDORS OF ALL SORTS, CARNIVAL BOOTHS, A GIANT STATUE OF A STANDING BLACK BEAR, THERE IS A FESTIVAL ATMOSPHERE.

ROBIN PRUFROCK COMES INTO VIEW, EATING COTTON CANDY.

PRUFROCK: Hi! This is Asbrignastat festival in Iceland. This is like the Bear Olympics! This is the place we've come to, to tell the next phase of our story.

FROM THE CROWD PASSING BY, SOMEONE CALLS...

PERSON IN CROWD: Robin? (Louder) ROBIN PRUFROCK??

PRUFROCK TURNS, VISIBLY SURPRISED: Abe? What are you doing here?

ABE WILKS STEPS OUT OF THE CROWD. THE TWO MEN SHAKE HANDS.

ABE WILKS: This is the big bear event. I always come here.

PRUFROCK: Okay, that makes sense. Yes. I see it. How long have you been here? We're still shooting? Okay, good. Are Abe's releases still good? Yes?

ABE WILKS: Are you still shooting your documentary? I thought you'd be done with that by now?

PRUFROCK: Yeah, it takes a long time. Hundreds of hours of footage, over months, and then editing it down. It's lengthy process. ... Listen Abe, you know your way around?

ABE WILKS: Pretty well. Coming here for years.

PRUFROCK: Cool. Want to hang out a bit. Show us around.

WILKS SHRUGS: Sure thing.

PRUFROCK: Ok, let me just wrap up my intro. (Turns to camera, clears throat) Okay! The Icelanders had domesticated the bear as the new food animal, but that's not where things stopped. There was another issue. Cattle and horses had declined in Iceland, and these were working animals. So there was an emerging shortage of draft animal labor. Sheep and goats couldn't quite fill the bill. There was a job vacancy.

QUICK CUT TO A MOTEL SIGN - A NEON WORD - VACANCY.QUICK CUT TO A SIGN IN A HOTEL WINDOW - HELP WANTED.

CAMERA FOLLOWS PRUFROCK AND ABE WILKS THROUGH THE CROWD

PRUFROCK: Everything is mechanized now, but in centuries past, Icelandic bears pulled plows, hauled carts and wagons, even carried riders.

PRUFROCK (TO ABE WILKS): Normally we expect that sort of thing from hoofed animals. With bears... It seems counterintuitive. How suitable were bears for that sort of thing?

ABE WILKS: Well, not my area. But I do know that bears in the wild are pretty damned strong. There's all kinds of strength though. Take tigers, they're really strong, but it's all short term. They're all about sprints and ambushes, and then they spend a lot of time resting. Horses and cattle, they're known for steady output. Marathoners, they'll put out a steady eight hour day, and that's what you need for farming or any kind of long distance. Anyone, anything can do a sprint, it's the ones that stick it out.

PRUFROCK: Where do bears fit in you think?

ABE WILKS: I don't really know. I know that bears are incredibly strong. A half grown can flip three hundred pounds with one paw, I think I was telling you that. But steady work? I do know that black bears in the wild can cross quite a bit of countryside when they're looking for food. There's cases of some travelling for a thousand miles and more.

PRUFROCK AND ABE WILKS ATTENDING THE DEAD PULL - BEARS DRAGGING LOADS ON SLEDS. THERE IS A HUNDRED YARD DISTANCE. EACH BEAR IN HARNESS, WEARING A MODIFIED HORSE COLLAR.

PRUFROCK: The collars are so that they don't choke. There was the same problem with horses. Basically, the collars redistribute pressure around the shoulders, rather than the chest and neck. With a horse collar, a horse collar can pull twice as much weight. But a bear's anatomy is different. Without a collar, a bear wouldn't be able to pull any weight at all.

THE STARTING GUN IS FIRED, THE BEARS SURGE FORWARD. THE LOADS ARE IMMENSE, PILED HIGH ON THE SLEDS, WITH ICELANDERS CLINGING TO THE SIDES, THE BEARS STRUGGLE FORWARD THEIR CLAWS DIGGING.

PRUFROCK: Each load is five thousand pounds, roughly eight times the weight of the Bear. The test is to see who can bring the load fastest. That's very impressive.

THE CAMERA FOLLOWS THE BEARS STRUGGLING RAPIDLY FORWARD IN A SERIES OF LUNGES, THEIR CLAWS TEARING UP THE GROUND. ONE REACHES THE FINISH LINE FIRST. THE CROWD GOES WILD.

NEXT EVENT, THE CART RACES, BEARS PACING AROUND A MILE LONG TRACK, DRAWING WOODEN CARTS. ROBIN IN THE CROWD, CHEERING ALONG. THE ANIMALS CANTERING.

PRUFROCK: We don't know whether a bear was first hitched to a cart or a plow. I think it was probably a cart. The people who owned bears probably didn't do a lot of their own plowing. If the horse collar hadn't made it to Iceland, it probably wouldn't have gone anywhere. But it must have worked out.

MONTAGE OF WOODCUTS - BEARS DRAWING TWO AND FOUR WHEELED CARTS AND WAGONS.

PRUFROCK: the first reference in literature or in art dates to 1362. But the practice must have been widespread before then.

CUT BACK TO PRUFROCK. CAMERA PANS OUT, REVEALING THAT HE'S SITTING IN A STURDY TWO WHEELED WAGON.

PRUFROCK: This is the bear sprint. I can't pronounce the Icelandic name for it. Three hundred yards, hell for leather. Bears train all year for this, we've got bears from all every town and village. This one of Halvi's bears, and he's going to let me race him. It's just one of the qualifying heat, and this bear, Snorli, has already made his numbers so I can't screw this up.

PRUFROCK LEANS DOWN, SPEAKING TO HALVI INGOLFS.

PRUFROCK: So, just hold the reins and let him go. Do I say Giddyap?

HALVI INGOLFS (heavily accented): You be fine. He is a champion, Snorli. He know what to do.

PRUFROCK: Snorli doesn't sound fast. Wish me ----

INCOHERENT NOISE, THE BEARS BURST FROM THE STARTING GATES. PRUFROCK IS WHOOPING WITH LAUGHTER. THE WAGONS ARE ALMOST BOUNCING FROM THE GROUND. THE CAMERA FOLLOWS THE RACE.

RACE OVER, PRUFROCK IS BEING HELPED DOWN FROM THE RACING CART. HE IS LAUGHING HYSTERICALLY. HIS FACE IS FLUSHED, HE IS COVERED WITH SWEAT.

PRUFROCK: What a rush. (laughs) I've never seen anything like that! My god. Just for a second, I thought I was going to die. I thought that. It was like being shot out of a rocket.

SOUND CUTS OUT ON PRUFROCK SPEAKING, AS IT GOES TO VOICE OVER.

PRUFROCK VOICE OVER I don't know who first hitched a bear to a cart, and I don't know when. But I know why. Just because.... Just because.... (chuckles)

****

OPENING, SCIENCE LABORATORY, BEAKERS AND COMPUTERS, LAB EQUIPMENT, BUNSEN BURNERS AND FLASKS. PRUFROCK IS MEETING WITH ZOOLOGIST/BIOCHEMIST DOCTOR FULLER MONHALTER.

FULLER MONHALTER: Pound for pound, a Siberian husky is the most powerful draft animal on earth. Dogs have pulled between 10 and 15 times their own weight in tractor pulls. A sled dog team can pull more than twice as much as a comparable horse team. They can carry a pack of up to 40% of their weight, compared to perhaps 13% for horses. Dogs are faster than horses over the long haul, capable of maintaining average speeds of eight to twelve miles an hour for hundreds of miles (including rest stops), and can exceed twenty miles an hour or more on shorter sprints.

PRUFROCK (ATTENTIVE): You're kidding, that's amazing.

FULLER MONHALTER: Isn't it though.

PRUFROCK: I'll never look at dogs in the same way. So why weren't dogs plowing our fields and drawing our carriages?

FULLER MONHALTER: A couple of reasons. Dogs are smaller, so you need more of them, and just handling large numbers of animals complicates things.

PRUFROCK: So it's easier to wrangle two horses than twenty dogs?

FULLER MONHALTER: Quite. The other issue is that dogs are much more expensive to maintain. They're meat eaters or omnivores, and that's an expensive diet. Horses eat grass, and normally, grass is very cheap.

PRUFROCK: That's why we see sled dogs in the north only?

FULLER MONHALTER: Go past a certain point, you run out of grass. Horses become very expensive to feed. And it's easier to feed dogs off the land. As a general rule, you only see the alternate domestics where the environment is not conducive to horse and cattle.

PRUFROCK: Okay, but let's compare animals. What's the horsepower of a horse?

FULLER MONHALTER (raises his eyebrow): About just under one horsepower for sustained work. That's why we call it horsepower?

PRUFROCK: Oops! I didn't quite get that. But now that you say, it's obvious.

FULLER MONHALTER: That's sustained labor. But with short bursts, as much as 15 horsepower.

PRUFROCK: And how is that compared to other animals - say cattle, water buffalo, camel, reindeer, goats, etc. and where do bears fit.

FULLER MONHALTER: There are several answers to that, and it all depends on how you look at it. A dog can carry 40% of its body weight, and a horse can carry only 13%. But a hundred pound dog will only carry 40 pounds and a thousand pound horse will carry 130 pounds. Elephants, pound for pound are relatively weak, but they're so large compared to other animals that they can move far more weight.

There's different things to consider. What kind of work is the animal doing? Carrying a pack is not the same thing as pulling a load. And even when you're pulling a load, the amount of resistance makes a difference - drawing a cart is different from dragging a plow through the earth, and even dragging a plow can be different depending on how deep you plow.

And then there's the ability to sustain work, and at what level. How do you compare an animal that can do light work for 20 hours, with an animal that can do heavy work, but only for four hours?

PRUFROCK (DUBIOUSLY): Sounds complicated.

MONHALTER: Sorry. There are a lot of variables to consider.

PRUFROCK (LAUGHS): It's okay.

PRUFROCK: The question is, how do bears rank as a working animal?

FULLER MONHALTER: Some ways good, some ways not so good. Take pack loading. The big winners there are dogs at 40% of body weight, reindeer at 30%, camels and yak at 25%, horses and cattle at about 13%, elephants at 8%. Bears are tested close to yaks or camels, say 20 or 25% of body weight, give or take.

PRUFROCK: Which makes them pretty good.

FULLER MONHALTER: But then, you're looking at animals that weigh running from 50 pounds to 5000 pounds. So your choice is a balancing act between the size of the animal and how much it weighs. A bear is pretty big, bigger than a dog or a reindeer. But much smaller than cattle. On average, a bear is maybe half the size of horse or cattle, so capable of carrying a comparable load. So if you look at it like that, then bears are about the same. But since cattle and horses are our default, the 'go to' or 'happy median' you have to say that bears are pretty competitive. Bottom line, you'd take a bear as easily as a horse to do your work.

Now let's look at other qualities, drawing a load or pulling a plow. Once again, bears are at the upper end of the scale, and as mid-sized animals, this makes them comparable to other big domesticates, not exact, but comparable.

So take a bear, a bear is strong enough to drag a much deeper plow than a single ox can. So effectively, a bear is exerting almost the force of a pair of oxen. A little less, but that's ballpark. But a bear doesn't have the same endurance, so while an ox might work steadily for six hours, a bear is maybe four. In a day, it might get half the acreage plowed as a pair of oxen.

PRUFROCK VOICE OVER, AS HE NODS ATTENTIVELY: I almost understood that.

PRUFROCK: So you could say that in terms of plowing a field, a bear is equivalent to an ox.

FULLER MONHALTER: You could say that, but it would be inaccurate.

PRUFROCK LOOKS HELPLESSLY AT THE CAMERA.

MONHALTER: There are differences between species capacities that makes it all apples and oranges. A camel, for instance, can plow more field than a pair of oxen working in tandem. Which you would think makes the camel, on average, more than twice as productive as a single ox. But plowing a field is working against considerable resistance, so a single ox might not be able to plow half of what a pair of oxen would. Its production might be much less.

PRUFROCK: My head hurts. (Pantomiming a headache)

MONHALTER: Oh it's really quite simple once you get the hang of it...

PRUFROCK: If you were to boil it down, you could say that in terms work output, pulling a plow, a bear is roughly the same ballpark as an ox.

FULLER MONHALTER: Well....

PRUFROCK: Work with me, please.

FULLER MONHALTER: If it was two bears pulling a plow. Really, the thing is that the sort of people who had bears were often the sort of people who owned oxen, and as far as uses, pulling a cart or a wagon was seen as having more status than pulling a plow. So they would prefer to use oxen.

Unless they were making some sort of point, or they didn't have anything else available, or they had to use whatever was at hand. Maybe you used the bear to plow light fields, and the oxen to plow deeper.

There was a certain amount of status involved, so you wanted people to see your bear working.

PRUFROCK: So in terms of....

FULLER MONHALTER: You didn't actually see wide scale use of bears for agricultural labour until about after the Laki Volcano erupted in 1783...

PRUFROCK: Wait... wait... I thought it was use for food, then for hauling carts and carriages, then for plows, then for riding and cavalry. I thought that was the logical progression...

FULLER MONHALTER: Oh no. I mean, it's rather more complicated.

PRUFROCK: Cut!

CUT TO, ROBIN PRUFROCK IN AN EDITING ROOM. TALKING TO PAUL BJORNSON. IMAGES PLAY ON THE EDITING SCREEN.

PRUFROCK: That was harsh. Three hours, and we've got maybe five minutes useable footage. He's not a bad guy, but he's talking way above our level.

PAUL BJORNSON: Well, maybe it's not that bad. Boil it down, I mean, people just need a broad sense of things. And we can flesh it out with some graphics and tables.

PRUFROCK: Graphics, sure. But I hate graphs and tables. This is a documentary, not a quarterly financial report.

PAUL BJORNSON: You've got some complicated information you want to get across. Do you want to just dump it? We can figure out something else.

PRUFROCK: Maybe. No.

PAUL BJORNSON: Do you want to go and spend another three hours talking to him?

PRUFROCK GIVES BJORNSON A LONG HARD STARE.

PRUFROCK: Let's do the graphs and tables.

CUT BACK TO INTERVIEW.

PRUFROCK: So broadly where do bears stand as a productive animal?

FULLER MONHALTER: They're right up there, with oxen certainly. It's not exact, you have to allow for different variables, but roughly, I'd put camels at the top, then horses, then oxen, then bears, then–

CUT TO ANIMATED GRAPHIC - A CAPTION READS - "HORSEPOWER PER ANIMAL" THEN A SUCCESSION OF ANIMATED CREATURES APPEAR ON THE SCREEN, ONE AFTER ANOTHER, ACCOMPANIED BY A RED POWER BAR,

INDICATING POWER LEVEL. AT THE TOP OF EACH POWER BAR IS A NUMBER.

> *CAMELS - 1.30*
> *WATER BUFFALO 1.15*
> *HORSE - 1.00*
> *YAK - 0.90*
> *OX - 0.80*
> *BEAR - 0.75*
> *REINDEER - 0.60*
> *MULE - 0.50*
> *DONKEY - 0.30LLAMA - 0.25*
> *MAN - 0.10*

CUT TO PRUFROCK IN EDITING SUITE WITH BJORNSON.

PRUFROCK: That's a terrible graphic.

PAUL BJORNSON: You want to talk to him for another three hours instead, and see if you can get some useable quotes?

CUT BACK TO PRUFROCK INTERVIEWING DOCTOR MONHALTER.

PRUFROCK: So if bears are relatively good workers, then why is bear domestication mostly Iceland and Scandinavia.

FULLER MONHALTER: You mean, apart from the fact that they're bears, Mr. Prufrock?

PRUFROCK (DOUBLE TAKE): Did you just make a joke?

FULLER MONHALTER: About a large immensely strong predator four or five times the size of a human being? I think the better question is why they were domesticated in Iceland at all. It was a fluke.

PRUFROCK: Let me put it another way. Why Iceland? Why didn't bears domestication catch on there and nowhere else?

FULLER MONHALTER: Ah, I see. Two reasons. First, we already have domesticates who are very well established. Horse and cattle have been domesticated for thousands of years, so it's hard for a new product to break into the marketplace as it were. People stick with what they know, and bear labor isn't nearly a big enough advantage to make them change their ways. By the same token, we had many meat animals - cattle, horse, sheep, pigs, etc., so under normal circumstances we didn't need a new one. Iceland was simply not normal circumstances.

PRUFROCK: And the other reason?

FULLER MONHALTER: Economics. Bears have a relatively expensive diet, particularly compared to horse and cattle which eat grass. They're similar to pigs in diet. Our global civilization is mainly grass and grain based, so it gives horse and cattle a tremendous advantage, particularly for draft. We do establish other domesticates, but only where horse and cattle are at a serious disadvantage.

CUT TO SPINNING MAP OF THE GLOBE - GRINNING ICONS OF HORSE AND CATTLE SHOW UP ALL OVER EUROPE, ASIA, THE AMERICAS. THEN THEY REDUCE IN SIZE. AS THE GLOBE SPINS, ARROWS APPEAR OVER CERTAIN REGIONS

NEW CARTOON ANIMALS POPPING UP, WITH ACCOMPANYING SUBTITLES:

DOGS - ARCTIC CANADA

REINDEER - SUBARCTIC RUSSIA

CAMELS - SAHARA AND GOBI DESERT

YAK - TIBETAN STEPPE

WATER BUFFALO - SOUTHEAST ASIA RAIN FOREST

LLAMA- ANDES MOUNTAINS

THE SPINNING GLOBE STOPS, AND SWINGS UNTIL ITS OVER ICELAND

BEARS - VIKING ICELAND.

CUT TO PRUFROCK AND BJORNSON, PRUFROCK IS SHAKING HIS HEAD.

PAUL BJORNSON: So what's the plan?

PRUFROCK: Hope they wake up? At least it's done.

****

MONTAGE: Scenes of Iceland, medieval scenes, village, people walking in old time costume. Suddenly, everyone stops and points. Everyone is looking. A well dressed man in a floppy hat rides into frame on a bear. The bear is in saddle and bridle, it walks along patiently. The camera follows the bear and rider as they go past, panning, panning.... until it comes to rest on ROBIN PRUFROCK holding a sign which reads "Dramatic Re-Enactment."

PRUFROCK: We don't know the date the first bear was born in Iceland in captivity, and we don't know the date that the first bear was hitched to a cart, or hooked up to a plow. But we do know the exact time, place and date that Snolli Stighasan strapped a saddle and bridle on to a bear and rode one for the first time ever.... June 10, 1348, in the village of Hvoltsvuller.

CAMERA - follows the bear and rider down the road, ambling casually.

CUT TO - FLASHBACK - Man cinching a saddle to the Bear and hooking a bridle.

PRUFROCK VOICE OVER: The story goes that Snolli, a local landowner, was late for an important meeting with his fellow landowners, and his horse was sick. So he hitched a wagon up to his black bear, as was often the custom back then, and started riding into town. But then the wheel broke on the cart...

CUT TO - Man standing beside cart with wheel off, bear sitting in traces, looking at him. In frustration he kicks the wagon, and then hops around holding his injured foot.

PRUFROCK VOICE OVER: So he saddled up, and the rest is history...

CUT TO - PRUFROCK back in the village, standing in front of a crude statue of the man riding a bear.

PRUFROCK: This statue commemorates that glorious event. .... Although, I have to wonder, what was he doing with that saddle in the first place.

CUT TO - Long short of the man on the bear, as they walk away from the camera. ZOOM IN - Man turns on the bear to look back at the camera, knowing smile on his face.

PRUFROCK: There's an alternate version of history here, in which some suggest that Snolli may have had this in mind for quite some time, that he'd been practicing in secret, and that he had a saddle specially made for the event, before the big reveal. Maybe that's true, maybe it's not, but I appreciate showmanship.

PRUFROCK begins to walk through the town. He passes another different man wearing a renaissance hat with ostrich feathers sticking out of it, and also riding a bear. The two of them nod to each other. PRUFROCK turns back to the camera.

PRUFROCK: The important thing was, that if he was the first, he wouldn't be the last.

ANOTHER MAN riding a bear goes past, this time in the opposite direction. He waves at PRUFROCK, who waves back.

PRUFROCK: It was going to catch on...

CAMERA pulls back and back, showing the village square, a half dozen bear riders in evidence, one of them dismounting to tether up his bear and go into a building.

PRUFROCK: Now it's true that for a lot of reasons, it's simply a lot easier and more convenient to ride a horse than it is to ride a bear, but riding a bear had one good thing going for it.... (Dramatic pause)

ZOOM IN ON PRUFROCK'S FACE, He's wearing a huge grin:

PRUFROCK: It's just so damned COOL!

PRUFROCK PUTS ON A COWBOY HAT, Takes three steps to a waiting saddled bear, and mounts up as if he's been practicing all day (which he has).

VOICE OVER, PRUFROCK WHISPERING TO HIMSELF: Okay, now how do I make him go?

MONTAGE - MEDIEVAL woodcuts of bear riding. Image of a man on a bear, with women and priests kneeling. Two men on bears fighting. A woodcut of a man fallen off, the bear rearing up, wearing an empty saddle.

PRUFROCK VOICE OVER: It caught on. It really was cool. Soon.... or within a generation or two, which in the Middle

Ages is like ultra-fast, everyone who was anyone was riding a bear. People were designing special saddles and bridles, some of them were real works of art. There were monographs being written on how to do it. It was in the artwork. Over in Hjalmsmir there is a church with a stained glass window, of Christ riding a bear the size of Godzilla. It was a fad, sure. But it caught on.

PAN BACK TO THE VILLAGE SQUARE, PRUFROCK APPEARING TO RIDE A BEAR, HIS SHOULDERS SWAYING AS HE THE ANIMAL WALKS.

PRUFROCK: It was a status thing. Bears. Tame bears, had always been a huge status thing. And in Iceland, bears were the province of the rich and famous, the wealthy and powerful, or at least those looking to make an impression.... or whatever Iceland had back then that passed for that.

There was a 'bear culture' among the social set - breeding bears, eating them, showing them off, and then showing them off doing tricks, hauling carts, etcetera. There was an entire group of people who had these things, and they were always trying to one up one another...

CLOSE UP OF PRUFROCK, STILL SWAYING, THE BACKGROUND SLOWLY SHIFTING, WITH THE ANIMAL UNDER HIM. HE IS SMILING.

PRUFROCK: And showing up riding one like a pony, that was upsmanship!

CAMERA PULLS BACK - PRUFROCK isn't actually riding a bear. He's on a saddle frame mounted on a cart, a couple of technicians have been moving the saddle, to simulate the rocking of an animal, while another pair of technicians pull the cart forward.

CLOSE UP - PRUFROCK winks at the camera.

****

CUT TO - THE BEAR FESTIVAL. PRUFROCK is sitting in stands, about to watch the bear races. Cut to the starting gates opening, bears and bear jockey's stampeding out.

PRUFROCK: Go, go, go!!! (He whoops loudly) This is just like horse racing, but with bears! (Grins at the camera). Of course, not every bear could be ridden like a pony, just the big ones. But this was the nobility, they had been selecting for size.

CUT TO TOM HAGGERTY, IN A WHITE COAT AND IN A LAB SOMEWHERE: The Icelandic breed is the largest of the American Black Bears. They're derived almost entirely from the Labrador black bears, some of the largest wild stock, and have gotten bigger. Males regularly go seven hundred pounds. And the largest ones are a match for the largest Black Bears anywhere.

BACK TO PRUFROCK - Watching the races.

PRUFROCK: Look at them go (Shouting into the camera now, to make himself heard over the roar of the crowd). In the game of one upsmanship, you've always got to keep on coming up with the next thing. Bear riding was a huge status thing. Nothing said 'Important and Dangerous' like riding up on a bear.... Not that it wasn't without risk.

CUT TO WOODCUT OF A SADDLED BEAR TEARING APART HIS FORMER RIDER.

PRUFROCK: But the risk actually made it more appealing.... It was the ultimate statement. You had to be fearless to ride a bear, and everyone knew it.

The Bear Cavalry — Page 75

QUICK CUT TO SEAN CONNERY as James Bond, sitting at a table in Casino Royale, coolly making his play, saying "Hit me."

CUT TO PRUFROCK

PRUFROCK: But of course, after a while everyone... Well, not everyone, but everyone who was rich enough who wanted to look tough: They were riding a bear. And then you were getting into bear races, to see who could go the fastest, and competitions, and bear battles. Bear battles were definitely a thing.

CUT TO WOODCUT - Two rearing bears fighting each other.

PRUFROCK: And ultimately to bear cavalry.

THE CROWD GOES WILD, QUICK CUT, THE RACE HAS BEEN WON. THE ROAR OF THE CROWD IS DEAFENING. PRUFROCK STANDS UP AND CHEERS.

****

PRUFROCK IS LEANING ON A FENCE. There's some sort of contest going on, the cheering is raucous, but he is not joining in.

PRUFROCK: It wasn't all fun and games. There was a dark side to Iceland's love affair with black bears.

MONTAGE - WOODCUT imagery of bears fighting each other, bears fighting dogs, in pits, with onlookers cheering, chained bears being tormented by men with spears. It gives way to savage paintings, then comic panels, clips from black and white films. Violent footage.

PRUFROCK VOICE OVER: It was a darker age, and blood sports were popular. Dogfighting, bullfighting, bear baiting, bear gardens, these were all part of medieval life. The Icelanders sometimes battled their bears against each other, or pitted them against dogs for sport. There's at least one account of a black bear facing a captured polar bear in a pit. (Background music of violence, grunts and bellows, cries of pain rising) It was ironic, the Icelanders were working so hard to domesticate their bears, make them docile.... When it was time to have them fight, they had to work hard at it. There are written descriptions on how to make a bear savage.

VOICE OVER - AN OLDER VOICE, ICELANDIC ACCENT, CLEARLY READING FROM A TEXT: .... To render savagery upon the beast, it is good to starve it, but not so much as to weaken its vigor. Curses of god you may shout upon it, and prick it many times so it gains no rest. Fire is its terror, but burns light upon its hide will rouse it to fury...

CUT TO PRUFROCK, still leaning on fence, looking out on the event.

CUT TO TWO BEARS, THEIR PAWS SHEATHED IN PADDING, WEARING MUZZLES, ONE WEARING A RED HARNESS THE OTHER YELLOW, REARING AND RUSHING AT EACH OTHER TO GRAPPLE WHILE THEIR HANDLERS URGE THEM ON.

IN THE BACKGROUND, SPECTATORS ARE CHEERING.

PRUFROCK: Maybe we haven't changed that much.

****

OPENING - AERIAL VIEW OF A CASTLE. CAMERA SWEEPS DOWN, PASSING THROUGH PALATIAL

The Bear Cavalry – Page 77

HALLS. ROBIN PRUFROCK on a throne in a palace, wearing royal robes and a Hollywood crown. He sets the crown on the arm of the throne. He looks at it for a second and then turns to the camera.

PRUFROCK: The thing about history, is that time after time, it's stuff that is happening somewhere else that eventually works its way over to you.

Iceland was about as far away and remote as you could get and still technically be a part of Europe. The Viking era was over, no one was sailing the North Atlantic, and their closest neighbor, Greenland, had pretty much faded away, forgotten. Iceland was almost forgotten. The world had moved on.

CUT TO - CGI GRAPHIC OF EUROPE - Centered on Germany and France, the camera pulls back showing more and more of the map, until finally Iceland appears in the top left hand corner. A cartoon arrow points to Iceland with the graphic: "Really really far away."

CUT BACK TO PRUFROCK.

PRUFROCK: Sure, the Icelanders had a civil war back in the day, and everyone went around armed with swords and axes ready to do battle, but really, they were basically doing the minimum you needed to do to be a Viking. The Icelanders had never been raiders.... there was just no one out there to raid.

CUT TO PAUL BJORNSON, THE BEAR, Dressed as a Viking, still with only one horn on his helmet, holding his rubber sword in an empty field of desolate rock, looking around hopefully...

CUT BACK TO PRUFROCK ON THE THRONE.

PRUFROCK: In 1262, Iceland became part of the Norwegian Crown.

Most Norwegians didn't really notice. For about a hundred and fifty years, no one really paid any attention to Iceland.

The Little Ice Age had hit, and things got worse and worse all over Scandinavia. Norway had its own problems with the little ice age, population was dropping, the political independence and status of the Norwegian monarchy was in decline.

On July 21, 1336, Magnus Erikkson became king of Norway and Sweden, crowned Magnus IV, a Kingdom that included Iceland and Greenland, and bits of Finland and Denmark.

CUT TO ROYAL PORTRAIT OF MAGNUS ERIKKSON.

THEN CLOSE UP OF A MAP OF SCANDINAVIA AND NORTHERN EUROPE. CONTINUING SERIES OF SHOTS INTERCUT, YEAR TO YEAR, WITH PROVINCES TURNING RED OR BLUE, DEPENDING ON ACQUISITIONS OR REBELLIONS.

PRUFROCK VOICE OVER: Magnus Erikkson was succeeded by his son, Haakon IV.

CUT TO ROYAL PORTRAIT OF HAAKON IV. THEN BACK TO YEAR BY YEAR CHANGES ON THE SCANDINAVIAN MAP.

PRUFROCK VOICE OVER: In 1363, he married ten year old Margaret of Denmark.

CUT TO ROYAL PORTRAIT OF MARGARET AS A YOUNG GIRL.

PRUFROCK VOICE OVER: ...whose father was the king of Denmark.

CAMERA PULLS BACK, SHOWING THE PORTRAIT OF MARGARET IS A LARGER PORTRAIT OF HER AND HER FATHER.

PRUFROCK VOICE OVER: He died in 1380, but before he died, Margaret had consolidated her claim to all three thrones by having her son Olaf appointed as Haakon's heir, to the crowns of Norway and Denmark, with Margaret acting as regent for all three kingdoms. Olaf died in 1387, but somehow, Margaret held onto power, appointing her grand-nephew as Olaf's replacement.

CUT TO ROYAL PORTRAIT OF MARGARET OF DENMARK, NOW FULLY MATURE,

THEN BACK TO PRUFROCK, ON THE THRONE. HE STEPS OFF THE THRONE. CUT TO HIM WALKING DOWN A PALACE HALLWAY, PAST ROYAL PORTRAITS OF KINGS AND QUEENS. HE LOOKS AT THE CAMERA.

PRUFROCK: Now this is the simplified version - what was going on were rebellions all over the place, civil wars, kingdoms were divided up, or pawned off, there were wars with the Germans, wars with the Russians, pretenders to the throne. You would need a scorecard to keep up with it all.

And by and large, the Icelanders didn't. It was all a lot of bother, a long way away, and while technically, they were part of somebody's kingdom, it didn't seem to matter all that much. All these wars, all these intrigues were happening a long way away, to other people.

ZOOM IN ON PRUFROCK, STANDING IN FRONT OF MARGARET'S FINAL ROYAL PORTRAIT.

PRUFROCK: The ultimate result of all of Queen Margaret's maneuvering was the Treaty of Kalmar in 1397, This was the beginning of the Kalmar Union, which stipulated an 'Eternal Union of the Three Kingdoms' - Denmark, Norway and Sweden, and also including Finland, Iceland and Greenland. Vinland, technically, although by that time, everyone had pretty much given up on Vinland, no one cared about Greenland and almost no one cared about Iceland. But it was all united 'under a single king.'

CUT TO MAP OF SCANDINAVIA, OPENING UP TO INCLUDE ICELAND AND GREENLAND, TURNING COLOUR TO RED, SHOWING THE BOUNDARIES OF THE KALMAR UNION.

BACK TO PRUFROCK.

PRUFROCK: If you weren't Margaret of Denmark, running the Kalmar Union was not an easy thing. The way it was set up, it was essentially like trying to ride three horses at once. Three horses that didn't like each other, and tended to want to ride off in different directions, or have it out with each other. Technically, they were still three kingdoms, just one king, so it was sort of royal multi-tasking, or maybe a blue blood version of polygamy - polykingamy? The fifteen year old, Eric of Pomerania was crowned king, but actually, Margaret continued to run the show:

CUT TO ROYAL PORTRAIT OF THE FIFTEEN YEAR OLD ERIC OF POMERANIA.

CUT BACK TO PRUFROCK, ROAMING THROUGH THE CASTLE. HE STOPS TO TAP ON A SUIT OF ARMOUR.

PRUFROCK: Now, Eric was in an interesting position. He'd actually been proclaimed as King of Norway back when he was seven years old. Then at fourteen, he'd been proclaimed as King of Denmark. And finally, the triple crown in 1397.

He had been a king since before he hit puberty, but he had never ever been allowed any power, and he wouldn't really have power until Margaret passed on.

In 1397, he was fifteen years old, and probably typical for any fifteen year old boy, except for the being king part. That meant that he was short tempered, impulsive, stubborn, boiling over with hormones, frustrated and irresistibly attracted to cool things.

And he did something which no Norwegian king had really done in a hundred and fifty years: He noticed Iceland!

Actually, he noticed the bears.

The bear fashion was long gone in Scandinavia by this time. But bears remained a potent part of culture and folklore. Bears were a symbol of strength and power, and that would have been compelling to a boy king who had the title, but was powerless.

Eric got interested in bears, he read of Polar bear cubs being given as gifts a century earlier. He wanted one.

In 1399, the hint was dropped very strongly that if Iceland wanted to show their new seventeen year old King proper respect, they'd ship over a polar bear for him to play with.

MONTAGE OF BEAR WOODCUTS, MOVIE CLIPS, ETC.

PRUFROCK: As it turns out, the Icelanders couldn't actually lay their hands on a polar bear. Polar Bears weren't native to Iceland. They showed up once in a while riding in on the ice floes, but you couldn't count on that. For polar pears you had to go to Greenland or beyond. By this time the Greenland settlement was pretty much on its last legs and they weren't in shape to help out.

So they did the next best thing - they found a whitish/blond bear cub.... There are such things....

And they shipped that over, hoping that the King of the Kalmar Union wouldn't know the difference.

And he didn't! By all accounts, Eric swallowed it whole. He loved his bear cub, and took it everywhere with him as a pet. Eric had the cub for two and a half years before it died of a sudden illness.

Some say that Margaret had it poisoned, she wasn't a big fan at all. Anyway, it probably worked out for the best, because a spoiled rotten full grown bear? Well, sooner or later, something bad was going to happen.

PRUFROCK STOPS AND LOOKS UP. CAMERA MOVES TO SHOW WHAT HE'S STARING AT.

ANOTHER ROYAL PORTRAIT, THIS ONE OF ERIC AND HIS BEAR. CAMERA LINGERS ON THE BEAR.

PRUFROCK VOICE OVER: Eric was heartbroken. In 1403, he wanted another one. This time, Margaret put her foot down. The first one, she had gone along with. If he was playing with the bear, it kept him out of trouble, and best of all, it kept him from asking for awkward things, like being treated as the King and being allowed to go to cabinet meetings and make decisions.

But another one.... That was a bit much.

CUT BACK TO PRUFROCK, ROAMING THE CASTLE, PEERING AT MEDIEVAL TAPESTRIES AND WEAPONS.

PRUFROCK: I have the impression that Margaret had gotten really really really sick of having the thing around those years. And she had gotten more and more worried as it grew that maybe having large dangerous predator roaming the grounds was not a good idea. There had been a few .... 'incidents.' (makes air quotes).

Now, since 1399, Eric's fondness for bears had only increased. He read up on Icelandic Bear carts and bear riders, he'd read of the old bear-shirt Vikings. He probably put up woodcuts on his bedroom wall. He was a complete bear maniac, the way kids from my Dad's time were car maniacs, and kids from my son's time are computer maniacs. He had even had a saddle shipped over from Iceland, planning to ride his bear when it was old enough.

PRUFROCK pauses, reflecting.

PRUFROCK: That probably wouldn't have turned out well.

PRUFROCK SHRUGS.

PRUFROCK: So, to say that Eric took Margaret's refusal to let him have another bear well is probably an understatement. Apparently, Eric threw an epic tantrum that is still famous today.

Margaret stood firm, there was nothing that Eric could do about it.

He did keep asking though, and Margaret kept refusing. But Eric was famously stubborn, and he was determined to get his way. In 1405, he came up with a proposal that would prove he was not just a spoiled young man trying to get his way, but a King making a serious proposal on a matter of state. A proposal that Margaret could not say no to.

Bear Cavalry!

CUT TO A PAINTING OF BEAR CAVALRY IN BATTLE.

BACK TO PRUFROCK, CLOSE UP.

PRUFROCK: Well, of course she said 'No'

She wasn't stupid.

Maybe it's something in the water up there. Scandinavian royals seem to have a penchant for crazy ideas. In the 1600's, Charles XI of Sweden tried his hand at Moose Cavalry, that didn't turn out well EITHER.

Now maybe if Queen Margaret had said yes, and then proceeded to let the whole venture fall on its face, Eric would have gotten it out of his system.

But she said no, and Eric, being stubborn, just added it as one more item on the list of things that he was going to do when he actually allowed to rule as King in more than name.

Margaret died in 1412, and suddenly, Eric was in charge.

CUT BACK TO THE PAINTING OF BEAR CAVALRY IN BATTLE.

BACK TO PRUFROCK, ROAMING THE CASTLE.

PRUFROCK: Now, to be fair, Eric actually did get on with the business as governing. He was serious about being a good king. But he was also serious about doing all the things he had always wanted to do, and Bear Cavalry was on that list.

CUT TO ROYAL PORTRAIT OF ERIC AT 30 YEARS OF AGE, IN 1412....

****

OPENING - ROBIN PRUFROCK In a laboratory with Doctor Paul Watson, zoologist. His name and credentials flash across the scene. Both are wearing lab coats, and sitting at a high table. Watson is speaking rapidly but clearly. Occasionally the camera shifts to PRUFROCK who nods, but does not speak:

PAUL WATSON: Are the Icelandic bears a domesticated species? There's some debate about that. Generally, the rule is that the domesticated species is measurably different from the wild version. They may be larger or smaller, they behave differently. Domesticated species may reproduce faster or earlier. There's a number of things that we look for.

Morphologically, the Icelandic breed is quite close to the wild form. I don't think it would qualify as a subspecies. Many of its features are common with wild bears. They reach sexual maturity at around three years, full growth at five years. Gestation takes about 225 days, although there is delayed implantation for a couple of months after mating. Although these qualities are the same in both the wild bears and Icelandic bears, it's worth noting that these ranges are common for large domesticates - the horse has about the same maturation rate and a longer gestation period for instance.

One significant difference is that the Icelandic bears breed much more rapidly and often than the wild bears. This is almost certainly a result of human intervention. Cubs are taken as early as possible after weaning, and females become ready to breed thereafter. In the wild, a protracted period of cub care means that females do not breed as often.

The Icelandic breed differs from the wild North American breeds in a few particulars. They're consistently larger. Icelandic bears tend to cluster at the far end of the size scale for the Black Bears. Or the super-size scale - of the 15 recorded black bears that exceeded a thousand pounds, 12 of them have been Icelandic bears. You just can't wave that away, the Icelandic bears are a very distinctive population.

At least some of this greater size is probably inherited - the Newfoundland/Labrador subspecies that the Icelandic bears were derived from is the largest wild subspecies. And the result of selective breeding by Icelanders. However, we cannot discount the effect of diet and care. Pregnant bears are well fed, producing robust offspring. The Icelandic Bears are invariably much better fed and cared for, and avoid many of the injuries and parasites that they would be subject to in the wild. The size of Icelandic bears is probably a case of environment maximizing genetic potential.

The other big difference is behavior. This can be argued about, but the Icelandic bears have a reputation for being much more human tolerant, less excitable, more docile. They behave differently than North American black bears, even ones raised from birth in captivity. Now, is this inbred, has there been selection for docility? Or is this just better bear handling by Icelanders both as experienced individuals and as a culture? Or the bears themselves learning moderate behavior from other bears... We're not sure. But they're different.

The diet of Icelandic bears differs from that of wild bears. Generally, the Icelandic bears have more food available, particularly at critical life phases. In addition to plants, insects and fish, bears are fed human leftovers, particularly meat and fish by-products. One unusual feature of Icelandic bear diet is cooking - Bears are fed bear stew, large quantities of leaves or vegetable matter which is made edible by boiling or roasting, mixed with meat or fish to enhance the flavor. Although they are omnivores and eat vegetation, bears are not nearly as effective or efficient at digesting plant material, and don't have many of the adaptations of dedicated herbivores. So bear cooking substantially expands the range of edible materials for them. It's noted that wild bears have no difficulty with the same diet as Icelandic bears.

Genetically, the Icelandic bears are well within the ranges of the wild black bears. But's a little bit more complicated than that. That's not too surprising, since starting about the 1800's, the Icelanders began importing black bear cubs from North America to avoid inbreeding. So genetically, yes, it's going to resemble the wild population. But even there.... Earlier, the Icelanders tried to get around the inbreeding problem by breeding blacks with browns and polar bears. Mostly that didn't work, most of the hybrids weren't viable. But nevertheless, there's some genetic contribution from the other bears to the Icelandic genome, not much, maybe 5% to 8% and certainly not universal but it's there.

When the Icelanders started breeding wild bears back, they found the resulting offspring were a lot more aggressive than the bears they were used to. They learned a lesson fast, in those first decades and after that, they got a lot more careful. They imported a lot of bear cubs, even some adults, but they got pretty selective about which ones they allowed to breed.

CUT TO PRUFROCK, OUTSIDE THE LAB, ALONE. Addresses camera:

PRUFROCK: Did you get all that? That was just great. He was clear, articulate, organized. It was a lot of information in a short time, but it wasn't confusing at all. He had excellent camera presence. It's perfect. I don't think we need to edit it at all. Hell, we don't even need to spruce it up with cutaways. What do you think? Just run it straight?

****

The Bear Cavalry — Page 88

SCENE: PORTRAITS OF ERIC OF POMERANIA,
Opening young shot of him with pet bear, paintings of bears.
Eric's coronation at 15. Eric as De-facto emperor.

PRUFROCK VOICE OVER: In 1412, Queen Margaret died.
Erik of Pomerania at the age of thirty, for fifteen years King
in name, finally came to power as the undisputed king of
Norway, Sweden and Denmark, the Kalmar Union.

PRUFROCK, AGAIN WALKING THROUGH A
PALACE, PAST PORTRAITS AND STATUES OF
MONARCHS.

PRUFROCK: Now in fifteenth century Scandinavia, being a
king was not necessarily the best deal. The kingdoms were
each very insistent on being separate kingdoms, and their
interests were often quite different.

Denmark kept getting involved in wars with Germany, which
Sweden disliked because it interfered with their exports to the
same country.

Sweden clashed with Denmark.

Norway clashed with Sweden. Nobody got along.

Each country maintained its own Council of Nobles who
essentially elected their kings, and got to make laws and
policy. Not only did they elect the King, but they could
impeach him as well, if they didn't like him. The King was
restricted in what he was allowed to do. The Council had its
jurisdiction, the King had his.

It was like trying to ride three horses at once.

CUT TO RODEO SCENES OF TRICK RIDERS,
INCLUDING A MAN RIDING TWO HORSES.

BACK TO PRUFROCK.

The Bear Cavalry – Page 89

PRUFROCK: Not easy at all. Margaret could do it. She was one of the great rulers of her age. Eric, not so much. Waiting fifteen years had left him frustrated, angry and not entirely diplomatic. Eric's rule was going to be tumultuous.

By this time, Erik had matured a bit, he wasn't a teenager, he wasn't even a twenty-something. He had an entire country to play with now, that was a lot better than a bear cub. Still, after so many years under Margaret pitching bear cavalry... he could not let it go.

Now that he was really King, he was going to be a King with Bear cavalry.

PRUFROCK PICKS UP A LARGE PARCHMENT ROLL AND OPENS IT. PRUFROCK CLEARS HIS THROAT AND READS IN A FORMAL, FAUX BRITISH, VOICE: In our Royal Authority, we decree and authorize the enactment of an Icelandic Cavalry Unit of 500 stout men, equipped in all respects, and mounted upon the Bears for which Iceland is famous, as their contribution to the maintenance and defense of the Kingdom of Norway, as directed by the King.

PRUFROCK LOWERS THE PARCHMENT: This comes twenty-six days after the death of Margaret. It is one of the first official acts of Eric as the unquestioned ruler of the Kalmar Union.

PRUFROCK CLOSE UP: And everyone went... WTF?

STOCK FOOTAGE OF A GROUP OF VIKINGS IN A BAR, FREEZING WITH SHOCK.

PRUFROCK: Now, you have to understand, that Bear Cavalry back then existed only in the mind of a one frustrated royal, with a dubious grip on practicalities. And really, he was only pushing it because another royal wouldn't give him a pet bear and he was messing with her in revenge.

No one took it seriously, certainly no one in Copenhagen or Oslo or Stockholm. Especially, no one who was a serious soldier in Scandinavia. You had cavalry, you had musketeers, you had pikemen, you had infantry, you had sappers and sergeants, lieutenants and captains and generals. But men riding bears? Ridiculous!

But Eric had held onto the idea too long to let it go.

The trouble was that the legion of Bear Cavalry he summoned did not exist. The Icelanders didn't have an army, they didn't contribute legions or squadrons or anything to Norway or Denmark. They just went about doing their own things. Iceland had a lot of sagas filled with battles and brawling, but they hadn't actually had a war for 200 years.

So when the edict arrived on a ship... they just scratched their heads.

They didn't know what to do with it.

Heck, although there were a lot of domesticated bears in Iceland, and although some of them were used for labor, there were not five hundred riding bears in all of Iceland. There were probably not a hundred.

So, the royal edict went out in 1412... and nothing happened.

And then it went out again in 1413... and nothing happened.

By 1416, Eric was getting frustrated. This was starting to reflect back on his kingship. If some obscure far away province like Iceland could just ignore his edicts.... well, that wasn't good.

So he sent one of his best officers, Boguslaw of Silesia, out to Reykjavik to recruit and train his bear cavalry, a force of Five Hundred.

By 1419, he came back with twenty....

****

PRUFROCK: Now that might have been it. You can easily imagine these twenty men and their riding bears, sitting around for a while, not actually fitting in anywhere, until after a year or two they got sent home.

However, Eric was about to begin his great European tour.

This wasn't common, but it wasn't particularly unusual.

If you were a King, odds were at some point, you'd have to travel to see the Pope. You would visit other kingdoms, as part of alliances and negotiations.

In Eric's case, he had been married in 1406 to the King of England, Henry IV's daughter Philippa, as part of Margaret's plan for an alliance between England and the Kalmar Union.

So Erik had to go visit his father in law in England. And from there, he went to the Low Countries, or the Netherlands, and from there to France, stopping in Paris, and down to Rome to meet the Pope, stopping in at great cities along the way.

Back then of course, no one travelled alone. There was an entourage, men at arms, ladies in waiting, diplomats, physicians, personal chefs, servants and washerwomen, a personal guard... Eric ended up taking his bears with him.

Well, they were a sensation. Everyone was astonished. Tame bears were one thing. But this was a step beyond, a force of cavalry bears, ridden like horses, wearing armor. This wasn't real cavalry, this was more like Icelandic circus. By this time,

The Bear Cavalry – Page 92

Boguslaw had gotten them to ride in formation, had taught them enough military tactics that they wouldn't be a joke.... and of course these were some of the smartest animals in Iceland, so they knew all sorts of tricks.

Eric's bears were a hit in London. People travelled hundreds of miles to see them. The entertained the entire court. It was a circus.

And they took it seriously. Norway and Denmark was a long way away, these were exotic foreign lands. Travel and news simply wasn't as easy back then. The Europeans believed in dog headed men in Africa and Christian Kingdoms in Asia. If it was far away and strange... people bought into it.

So if Eric, coming from the exotic and foreign north, the land of the Vikings and the midnight sun, said that bears were the cavalry of Norway and the Kalmar Union...

Well, people just believed them!

CUT TO MONTAGE OF TAPESTRIES, WOODCUTS, SCULPTURES, MOSAICS, PENNY DREADFULS OF ALL KINDS, FEATURING VIKINGS AND BEARS.

This is really where it caught on. It starts in England, with this explosion of woodcuts and paintings, sculptures and tapestries, and all sorts of written, but entirely fabricated and fanciful, descriptions of the Vikings bear cavalry.

Within a generation, the English were retroactively adding bear cavalry into their descriptions and reports of the ancient Viking raids of a few centuries before.

Eric returned home to his Kingdom by 1421, but with his bear cavalry now firmly established as part of his retinue.

Boguslaw was sent back to Iceland to get more bears. Eric was determined to have his Cavalry unit. After all, he'd told the King of England all about it.

Within a couple of years, Eric decided to go on the road again, and from 1423 and 1425, he was proceeding across Europe, through Germany, the low countries, France and Italy.

By the time Eric got to France, everyone wanted to see his bears! Literally his entire path was paved with spectators. It was the topic everyone wanted to discuss. It was like a Katy Perry concert tour, but with more fur.

From France, into Italy. Even the Pope came to see the bears marching on the field, staging faked battles for amusement.

The Viking Bear Cavalry had irrevocably entered the western imagination...

****

OPENING SHOT - Rembrandt's famous 'Ragnarok' featuring the Norse Gods riding into battle mounted on Bears - Odin astride a huge rearing polar bear, wielding his spear. Thor and the other gods in various poses, riding an assortment of brown and black bears, all of them lunging forward into an unfolding darkness in the center of the painting. The camera pans across the painting, slowly moving from God to God. Slowly, the image gives way to a series of paintings and sketches, from 1500 onwards, coming with greater and greater speed, up to modern pulp magazine covers and movie posters.

PRUFROCK VOICE OVER: Eric of Pomerania's European tours had a quality of theatricality to it. You could almost say it was the first bear circus. But it introduced the idea of the bear cavalry to Europe, and somehow it caught on. At this point, there was no such thing, no bear had ever fought in battle. The whole thing was a near delusion. But it was a near delusion with legs.

CAMERA comes to rest on a painting of a huge bear in golden armor.

CUT TO - PRUFROCK, CAPTION READS, COPENHAGEN MUSEUM. PRUFROCK is in the back sections of the museum, away from the public exhibits. He is surrounded by tall shelving, wooden crates, there are large tables with arrays of objects being tagged and sorted. ROBIN is talking to an elderly man, the caption reads, Hans Podebusk. PRUFROCK is holding a large oddly shaped metal object in his hands.

PRUFROCK: So this is an authentic bear helmet, an actual piece of bear armor?

HANS PODEBUSK: Yes. Quite. And it was worn in battle, you can see the scour mark there? That is from a bullet. These scratches, probably from a knife or axe, they are very light, so it is quite likely that whoever made those marks did them at close quarters and in an unhappy situation. He probably did not live very long.

PRUFROCK: Wow. So, when was this worn?

HANS PODEBUSK: It is hard to say, we think probably around 1550.

PRUFROCK: So this really happened. There were armored bears charging into battle?

HANS PODEBUSK: Oh yes. There were a number of battles where they were deployed. The bear cavalry, during its day, was the closest pre-industrial civilization ever produced to a tank.

CUT TO - A FILM CLIP FROM A SWEDISH HISTORICAL FEATURE. A battle scene, 16th century, armored bears in the midst.

PRUFROCK VOICE OVER: The first use of Bear Cavalry was in 1426.

CUT TO - MAP OF KALMAR UNION. Map zooms in on Denmark, and then on the south of the Danish peninsula. The provinces of Schleswig and Holstein come into view.

PRUFROCK VOICE OVER: As if ruling three kingdoms and the territory of five modern countries wasn't enough, neither Margaret nor Eric could leave well enough alone. Both of them insisted on meddling in Germany. They fought with the Hanseatic League, tried to conquer Mecklenberg.

CUT TO - MAP - Mecklenberg glows on the German coast for a moment.

PRUFROCK VOICE OVER: But for Margaret, and especially Eric, the big prize were the provinces of Schleswig and Holstein. Literally, they were the gateway from Scandinavia and Denmark into the heart of Germany itself.

CUT TO - MAP - Close up of Schleswig and Holstein - showing Germany to South, Denmark and the southern tips of the Scandinavian peninsula to the North. A big red arrow makes its way down from Scandinavia into Schleswig and Holstein, splitting up into three arrows in Germany pushing left, right and down...

PRUFROCK VOICE OVER: The trouble was that these provinces were held by the Counts of Schaumburg and Holstein, and they weren't about to give up their lands.

CUT TO - Medieval portrait of a nobleman. Caption: Henry III, Count of Schaumburg and Holstein, Bishop of Ostabruck, Count of Holstein-Rendsberg.

PRUFROCK VOICE OVER: In 1403, as a result of the death of his brother Gerhard, Henry III, claimed the Duchy of Schleswig. Queen Margaret objected of course, wanting Schleswig for herself. In 1409 they went to war. In 1411 the war ended inconclusively.

CUT TO MAP - The arrows vanish, replaced by a big red X over Schleswig and Holstein.

PRUFROCK VOICE OVER: In 1412 Margaret died, and it was left to Eric to carry on. Eric's solution was very modern. He took them to court... and he won. But the Counts refused to give up the land.

CUT TO - PRUFROCK LOOKING WORRIED AND CONFUSED - turning over a piece of metal and staring at it. Podebust is with him helping. As the camera pans out, watching, it slowly becomes clear, as the narration goes on, that they are assembling a suit of bear armor onto a mounting frame.

PRUFROCK VOICE OVER: In 1419, he went to war.

QUICK CUT TO - PAUL BJORNSON, IN HIS BIG GAY BEAR VIKING OUTFIT, In his Viking helmet, rushing forward with sword upraised, soundlessly shouting a war cry.

PRUFROCK VOICE OVER: And in1420... he lost.

QUICK CUT TO - PAUL BJORNSON, staring forlornly at his bent rubber sword.

PRUFROCK VOICE OVER: Then he went on vacation, bringing his bears to Europe.

CUT TO INTERVIEW - ROBIN PRUFROCK in the office of the noted historian, Wilfred Whipple-Creme.

PRUFROCK: I don't understand this. So, Eric is completely enthusiastic about Bear Cavalry, an idea he's been pushing since he's a teenager. He's been in charge since 1412. He's ordered them practically the day he came to power.... and yet, here he is seven years later... where are they?

WILFRED WHIPPLE-CREME: Well, you have to understand. It was a stupid idea.

PRUFROCK - laughs.

WILFRED WHIPPLE-CREME: This was the obsession of a King, and that carried a great deal of weight. But Eric was nowhere near the omnipotent. He was surrounded by military men, by professional soldiers. These guys knew war, they had been fighting for most of their lives, some of them had been fighting for longer than he had been alive.

So you know, when he comes to them with this inspiration based on having a pet bear and some stories from Iceland about a cockamamie notion to have dangerous wild animals on the battlefield... well, they don't laugh in his face...

PRUFROCK: But let's say that they're not enthusiastic.

WILFRED WHIPPLE-CREME: To put it mildly. War is very serious business. He could order whatever they want, but there were a thousand different reasons to drag your feet without saying outright no.

By the time the war rolled around in 1419, Eric's Bears were only just arriving, there were only a couple of dozen, and Eric's generals were dead set against them being deployed at that point. The bears could be marched, they could be paraded, they could be trained... but actually in a battle?

No way. Eventually they would be deployed… but Eric was going to have to overcome that resistance.

CUT TO - PRUFROCK AND PODEBUSK have finished reassembling the Bear armor, which immediately collapses. PRUFROCK looks temporarily stricken, Podebusk laughing quietly.

CUT TO - Interview - PRUFROCK and Whipple-Creme.

PRUFROCK: 1426?

WILFRED WHIPPLE-CREME: 1426.

PRUFROCK: What's happening?

WILFRED WHIPPLE-CREME: Well, Henry IV and his brothers Adolph and Gerhard have been fighting the Kalmar Union off and on since Margaret's time. In 1423, hostilities had resumed.

PRUFROCK: But no bears were used in 1423?

WILFRED WHIPPLE-CREME: No. But by this time, one of Eric's chosen lieutenants, Boguslaw, had made several trips to Iceland, and he'd actually recruited a substantial number of bears and riders. But Eric was actually on travels through Europe at this time, and so the war was left in the hands of his psalters

PRUFROCK: And they were saying "No"

WILFRED WHIPPLE-CREME: Emphatically. But as it turned out, that was a good thing?

PRUFROCK: Why?

WILFRED WHIPPLE-CREME: It was like the Tuskegee Airmen? Ever hear of those? It was World War II, the US air force put together a corps of black airmen. But because of the racial policies of the day, no one wanted to send them into battle. So they were kept at home and put through training again... and again... and again... By the time they finally did get deployed, they were so much more experienced and trained that they were the best things in the air.

From 1421 on there was the prototype of bear cavalry, but Eric's generals were adamant about not letting them near a battlefield. They couldn't just say no to the King, so they had to keep on coming up with new reasons.

The bear cavalry riders needed armor, then the bears needed armor, they needed weapons, they needed training. Formal training at this time was basically unknown for soldiers, there was some, but it was expected you showed up ready to fight and learned on the job. So the fact that the bear cavalry was being trained and trained and trained was a novel thing.

PRUFROCK: So in 1425?

WILFRED WHIPPLE-CREME: In 1425, Eric returned back from his European travels.

PRUFROCK: And he wasn't going to take no for an answer?

WILFRED WHIPPLE-CREME: He wasn't. In fact, Eric had painted himself into a corner. He had taken a personal guard of bear riders across Europe with him, his bear cavalry had been the talk of the town in Antwerp, in Paris, in Milan and Rome.

Well, he was stuck, he'd put himself out there. It was put up or shut up. His prestige was on the line, he was either going to be taken seriously, or he was going to be another nutty royal, and there was no shortage of them.

This was the turning point. He couldn't allow his generals to keep making excuses.

PRUFROCK: And so the bears went to war?

WILFRED WHIPPLE-CREME: They did. Eric was 44 by then.

PRUFROCK: How did they do?

WILFRED WHIPPLE-CREME: They were devastating.

****

OPENING - Montage of stock footage medieval battle scenes, mixed with close ups of renaissance paintings and woodcuts, sounds of fighting and combat, whinnying of horses, grunts and roars of bears, metal on metal.

PRUFROCK VOICE OVER: Bear cavalry was first deployed August 25, 1425 at the battle of Flensberg.

CUT TO THE FIELD OF FLENSBERG, NOW A GRASSY MEADOW. THE FIELD HAS BEEN DECORATED WITH EXTRAS IN MEDIEVAL BATTLE GARB, LYING DOWN PRETENDING TO BE DEAD, VARIOUS PIECES OR PERIOD JUNK. SMOKE POTS OBSCURE THE VIEW. PRUFROCK IS WALKING ACROSS THE FIELD, CONDUCTION AN INTERVIEW WITH MEDIEVAL HISTORIAN, WILFRED HYDE-WHITE. THE CAMERA CLOSES IN...

PRUFROCK: What impact did Bear Cavalry have at Flensberg?

WILFRED HYDE-WHITE: At Flensberg, and at most of the other battles that took place through 1425 and 1426, they were considered decisive.

PRUFROCK: Why?

WILFRED HYDE-WHITE: One thing that is frequently overlooked was that the people doing the fighting were tired.

The Bear Cavalry – Page 101

The wars here had been going on for a couple of decades. The current conflict had been going on for two or three years already. On both sides, the soldiers were stressed, tired, malnourished, worn down. There was a lot of sentiment for just going home on both sides.

Into this, comes two new factors to drive the war into a new phase. First, Eric had returned from travels, and he was very demanding, very insistent on getting results, when by this time, neither side was all that interested in stirring the pot. So there was a new motivation from the Kalmar side.

The bear cavalry was the other new factor. They weren't just a new factor, they were fresh troops. And simply being fresh was a major factor when both sides were tired out. They were also very well trained, and during this time, any degree of training made a huge difference.

And they were bears...

PRUFROCK: And they were bears...

WILFRED HYDE-WHITE: On simple size, horses, especially the medieval cavalry horses matched bears pound for pound and frequently outweighed them. But bears were much more dangerous, on a sprint they could run down a horse, their paws had four inch claws and they could behead a man with one swipe, they had jaws and teeth that could crush bones. They could, literally tear a man, or a horse, limb from limb. And they could cross terrain that horses couldn't navigate. Their center of gravity was lower, and they were far more stable.

On these fronts, they were simply far more potentially dangerous than horse cavalry. A horse was simply a platform for the mounted cavalry men. A bear was a killing machine with a rider.

The Bear Cavalry – Page 102

Most significantly, horses were terrified of bears on the battlefield. This had been established during the long training period between 1419 and 1425, and it had been an excuse for not using them. But it turned out to be a factor that could be used effectively.

No horse would ever charge a bear, in fact a small number of bears could scatter a much larger number of horse cavalry. Having even token bear forces to deploy would devastate the enemy cavalry, simply by being there.

PRUFROCK: What about firearms? Rifles and muskets? Did they have them back then?

WILFRED HYDE-WHITE: Well, back then those things were quite new. In fact, this was before rifles, before muskets. What they had for firearms then were crude hand cannon - they weren't terribly accurate, they made a lot of noise and smoke. Arquebuses were coming in, they were matchlock firearms, a great improvement, and lighter and more portable. But even Arquebuses wouldn't do more than dent plate armor at long range... in fact one of the methods of testing plate armor back then was to fire an Arquebus at it.

At this period in Europe, these gunpowder weapons were still not very common, not very good and far from reliable. Military tactics had no idea how to use them. It wouldn't be until the military revolution in tactics around 1550 that they came up with the idea of firing them as volleys. Before that, what you had were small groups of individual Arquebusiers just firing however or wherever they went. Colorful, but not effective, and certainly in the 1420's, and for decades thereafter, little threat to bear cavalry.

PRUFROCK: So basically... they were indestructible.

WILFRED HYDE-WHITE: Well, they wore armor, they were very powerful and dangerous, and they and their riders were well trained. But indestructible... that's a bit much. If a firearm or an arrow got through their armor, that was it. Or they could be taken down by a squad of pikemen.

PRUFROCK: But if you had, say, a squadron, or a formation of them?

WILFRED HYDE-WHITE: Indestructible would be a very good word.

CUT TO STOCK FOOTAGE OF A MEDIEVAL BATTLE.

PRUFROCK VOICE OVER: In 1426, the war ended with the death of Adolph and the capture of Henry IV at Rendberg. As part of his ransom, Henry IV was forced to give Eric everything he demanded. Eric's crazy fantasy was vindicated, and the Kalmar Union was on the threshold of becoming a power in Germany.

CUT TO WILFRED HYDE-WHITE. CLOSE UP.

WILFRED HYDE0WHITE: In fact, the big challenge of bear cavalry was actually getting bears, notoriously solitary animals, to work in formation...

****

ROBIN PRUFROCK, SITTING BEHIND THE STEERING WHEEL OF A CAR, MUNCHING POPCORN.

PRUFROCK (ADDRESSING CAMERA IN THE PASSENGER SEAT): Now, as it turns out, most bear species are pretty solitary. But American Black Bears can be highly social. In the wild, they'll congregate around salmon runs, places where food is found. But anyone who has ever been to a small town garbage dump knows that bears don't mind hanging out together...

SUDDENLY, A BEAR APPEARS ON THE OTHER SIDE OF THE DRIVER'S SIDE WINDOW GLASS, HIS SNORT DAMPENING THE WINDOW, LOOKING CURIOUSLY AT ROBIN. PRUFROCK HOLDS UP THE POPCORN.

PRUFROCK: Want some?

POV FROM OUTSIDE THE CAR. CAMERA PULLS BACK, REVEALING THAT THE CAR IS ACTUALLY A JUNKED AND RUSTING WRECK. THE CAMERA KEEPS PULLING BACK, REVEALING THAT THE AREA IS A MUNICIPAL DUMP SITE, AND THERE ARE OVER A DOZEN BEARS SCAVENGING.

CUT TO - ABE WILKS, TALKING TO PRUFROCK.

ABE WILKS: Now black bears, they are gregarious if circumstances are right, and when they're around each other, they sort out their pecking order, which is mainly about who goes first and who gets out of the way.

But they're not particularly social. Not like dogs, you know, where they all work together and travel together and form a unit. Not like horses, or cattle, where you'll get a bull or a leader and everyone follows that one. Black Bears, they're not what you call team players.

PRUFROCK: I've heard that with big domesticates, the trick is that they have a social structure, and what humans do, is they take over and head up that social structure. That doesn't sound like it's happening here.

ABE WILKS: No, it's not like that at all. I think it's more like cats. Cats don't have social structure, but you see, the thing with cats, is that they think that their humans are their mother. That drives a lot of behavior. It's like that with the black bears, they can be pretty easygoing around each other, and even around dogs or humans, if they're used to them.

But bottom line is that they'll defer to a human like it's their mother. They're very loyal animals. Most of the time you hear of them getting in trouble, it's when their owner's not around, there's someone else getting into the picture.

PRUFROCK: So how did that work for Bear cavalry?

QUICK CUT TO 1950'S STOCK MOVIE FOOTAGE OF BEAR CAVALRY CHARGING.

CUT TO WILFRED HYDE-WHITE ON THE BATTLEFIELD.

WILFRED HYDE WHITE - Quite well actually. You see, the bears didn't have any social structure, they just deferred to their riders. That was who they paid attention to. Other bears, other soldiers, they wouldn't pay attention. So as long as the riders were well trained and coordinated, the bears were too.

PRUFROCK: But what happens if a rider gets hurt?

WILFRED HYDE-WHITE - Then that's probably a bad thing, because you've got a traumatized, panicked animal that can throw a man over a house with a swipe of the paw, and it may well be mad at the people it thinks killed its rider.

PRUFROCK: That doesn't sound good?

WILFRED HYDE-WHITE - Indeed. No one wanted to kill a rider. I've seen very explicit military orders for dealing with bear cavalry, and first and foremost was don't touch the riders unless they were very far from your troops. Kill the bear first, if you can, then after that, kill the rider if it suits you. But in battle, the only restraint was the rider, so you didn't want to touch him.

Sometimes, of course, even that didn't work. There are many, many instances of the animals panicking in the middle of battle, and then just tearing their way out of wherever they happened to be.

PRUFROCK: What would you do in a situation like that?

WILFRED HYDE-WHITE: Get out of the way. That was the only thing to do if a bear panicked in battle. The only person who was even minimally safe was the rider. They'd get off the bear, or just try and hang on, but after that, anyone unlucky enough to be in its path.... Well, it wouldn't be a good thing.

PRUFROCK: That doesn't sound like it would be useful on the battlefield.

WILFRED HYDE-WHITE: It depended. The generals, the riders, they knew what to expect from bears. Quite often tactics called for bear cavalry to engage with the enemy as quickly as possible, so that if they did panic, it would be the enemy lines they tore up. They worked with it.

****

OPENING - Montages of medieval scenes, portrait of Queen Phillipa, more portraits, palaces, ceremonies.

PRUFROCK VOICE OVER: Eric's victories in Schleswig and Holstein put him on top of the world, he was poised to drive into Germany.

PRUFOCK, BACK IN THE CASTLE.

PRUFROCK: But it wasn't going to last.

The Bear Cavalry – Page 107

For one thing, the wars were putting a lot of stress on the Kalmar Union. Denmark was all for conquering as much of Germany as it could get its hands on. But Sweden...

Sweden would get nothing out of conquest. Instead, Germany was their biggest trading partner, and these wars were hell on trade.

What held things together was another strong woman, his wife Philippa, the daughter of Henry IV of England. Philippa acted as regent for the Kalmar Union when Eric was travelling, but more than that, she was the de facto regent for Sweden a lot of the time.

In some ways, she was considered a better monarch than Eric himself, more focused on the task of governing. In many ways, Philippa was the glue holding Sweden in the union.

In January, 1430, Philippa died...

FILM CLIP OF A FUNERAL PROCESSION.

PRUFROCK, KNEELING IN THE CASTLE CHAPEL. THE CAMERA IS BESIDE HIM. HE TURNS TO LOOK AT IT.

PRUFROCK: After that, Eric's relationship with the Swedish Kingdom declined. By 1434, relations were so poor that farmers and mine workers began a national revolt. The Bear cavalry was used, but eventually Eric had to compromise.

This was followed by a peasant rebellion in Norway in 1436. Eric was able to put the rebellion down, but by this time Eric was 54, and getting tired.

He began to negotiate for his successor. Without children of his own, he wanted his cousin Boguslaw of Pomerania. At first, the Kingdoms of the Kalmar Union were resistant. Matters dragged on. In 1439, the Kingdoms of Denmark and

Norway agreed to accept Boguslaw. In 1441, Sweden finally agreed, and Eric just short of sixty years old, abdicated, to return to his ancestral position as Duke of Pomerania, the title formerly held by his cousin, with a small contingent of his prized Bear Guard.

CUT TO PORTRAIT OF BOGUSLAW.

PRUFROCK VOICE OVER: Boguslaw's rule was notable for fighting a peasant revolt in Jutland, in Northern Denmark, in 1441.

Again, Eric's Bear Cavalry was used to good effect, but it marked the third major occasion that the Kalmar kings used it against their own people.

CUT TO A CLOSE UP SCENE OF A RENAISSANCE PAINTING, AN ARMOURED BEAR IS SAVAGELY TEARING A SCREAMING PEASANT APART.

PRUFROCK VOICE OVER: Unfortunately, Boguslaw died by 1444. He was succeeded by Christopher of Bavaria, who ruled for years, dying in 1448. Christopher was replaced by Christian of Denmark, who ruled from 1448 to 1481.

CUT TO PORTRAITS, IN SUCCESSION, OF CHRISTOPHER AND CHRISTIAN.

****

CUT TO: Copenhagen Museum, Podebusk and PRUFROCK, looking at pieces of bear armor. PRUFROCK picks up a gigantic bear helmet, visibly struggling with the weight. The helmet is inlaid with bronze, giving it a golden sheen. Pieces of embedded glass make it appear to be jewel encrusted.

PRUFROCK: This one is huge.

HANS PODEBUSK: That is the helmet of Wotan.

PRUFROCK: Wotan?

HANS PODEBUSK: One of the biggest bears ever, during the reign of Christian I. We're actually preparing it to ship to the Bear Festival in Iceland. He's quite famous there.

PRUFROCK: Cool.

PRUFROCK tries on the helmet, it dwarfs him. QUICK CUT to ROBIN PRUFROCK's son trying on a Fireman's helmet. PRUFROCK and son in fireman's helmet walking off hand in hand.

PRUFROCK VOICE OVER: Eric of Pomerania was succeeded by Boguslaw, who was in turn succeeded by Christopher. In turn, in 1448, Christian I ascended to the Danish throne, but not to the Kalmar Union.

CUT TO PRUFROCK, OUTSIDE THE CASTLE, HAIR WAVING IN THE BREEZE.

PRUFROCK: The problem was that the Kalmar Union was more or less a voluntary association by three countries which only sort of got along. Each of the Kingdoms remained separate, each had their own aristocracies and parliaments which guarded their prerogatives jealously. Kings were elected... and if each could elect the same king, that was cool.

After four southern or Germanic rulers in a row - Margaret, Eric, Boguslaw and Christian, each having their power base in Denmark, the Swedes were getting pretty tired. All they were getting out of this union were wars with countries that they'd much rather be trading with.

So the Danes elected Christian. The Swedes elected Charles Knutson, also known as Charles II. Between them was Norway. For two years, Christian and Charles struggled for domination, eventually, in 1450, Norway elected Christian as king.

And after that, the war was on.

Between 1451 and 1456, Denmark and Sweden were at war with each other.

CLOSE UP OF PRUFROCK.

PRUFROCK: Initially, Eric's Bear Cavalry wasn't a factor. That had always been Eric's thing, and Eric had been gone for a decade. The Bear Cavalry had been used once during this period against a peasant rebellion. But by this time, mostly they'd been sent back to Iceland.

The Bear Cavalry was not well liked by the Horse Cavalry - that whole thing about Bears terrorizing Horses, well that applied to our side as much as their side. Bears had a reputation for being dangerous and unpredictable, and it was deserved. The army, left to itself, would just as soon not have them around.

Back in Iceland, the returning Bear Cavalry were treated as heroes. Mostly, they came home rich, and that counted for a lot since Iceland was by this time a fairly poverty stricken place. They came back with a lot of military experience, medals, fame and all that. And they came back networked. There were a lot of social connections that they made. All of this benefited Iceland as a whole. Instead of an unknown backwater, the Icelanders thought of themselves as almost a fourth Kingdom in the union, and in fact, later on, they would agitate for this status.

For the Icelanders, the returning Bear Cavalry were like rock stars. And well... just like rock stars, you wanted to see them perform.

****

CUT To Bear Festival in Iceland, crowds of people walking by. PRUFROCK is talking to a pretty tour guide.

GUIDE: The Asbrignnastat is very old, it goes back to 1440 or 1450. The soldiers, returning home with their war bears, they were very famous. Everyone wanted to see them. Well, the soldiers had to keep their bears fit for war, so they had to practice. So they would travel to practice with each other, and people would travel to watch them practice.

Even then, it was a big thing. The Asbrignnastat would travel around the country, and they would go from festival to festival. People would bring their own bears and train them to participate in the Asbrignnastat. Bears, they were not just to eat, it showed that. Even a common poor man, if he had a bear, and his bear was good, he could become famous and rich at the Asbrignnastat.

All the games we have now - the races, the bear fights, the battleball, this all comes from the Asbrignnastat.

****

CUT TO - Copenhagen Museum, Hans Podebusk talking to PRUFROCK while they fiddle with bear armor. Podebusk's dialogue is in English, but with subtitles.

HANS PODEBUSK: ....Iceland was boring back then. Really. It was a poor country, there was no tradition of theatre, there was little in the way of music, literature, art. There was just not enough wealth or population in Iceland to support any of that.

If you wanted to watch the ice floes form, well, there was that. And there was always watching the sheep. There was whatever peasants did to entertain themselves, but truthfully, there was not a lot to culture at this time in Iceland. All the culture was elsewhere.

So when the returning soldiers brought the Asbrignnastat with them, well... there was not a lot of competition.

PRUFROCK: So it got to be a big deal in Iceland?

HANS PODEBUSK: Yes

PRUFROCK: And what was the effect of this?

HANS PODEBUSK: Well, very simple. It militarized Iceland's bears. In 1416, it took Boguslaw of Silesia, one of Eric's best men, three years in Iceland to come up with twenty bears that could pass for pretend cavalry. It took ten years to build up even a token force that could go into battle.... But with the Asbrignnastat...

PRUFROCK: With the Asbrignnastat?

HANS PODEBUSK: You had hundreds ready pretty much whenever you needed to call them.

****

CUT TO - PAINTINGS OF MEDIEVAL WARFARE, Focusing on the war between Danes and Swedes, the profiles of Charles and Christians facing each other in opposition.

PRUFROCK VOICE OVER: Christian I of Denmark, and Charles II of Norway, by 1451 were going to war for the future of the Kalmar Union. Initially Bear Cavalry were not involved, the Danish military thought they were really more trouble than they were worth.

The war was fought mostly in Sweden and slowly began to devastate the countryside. By 1453, Sweden was bringing in mercenaries from Germany and Poland. Christian finally decided to call in the Icelanders and their bear cavalry. Almost a thousand showed up.

CUT TO - Paintings of armored bears rampaging among peasants, tearing apart a terrified knight, horses rearing eyes rolling in terror, the paintings have a disturbing brutal quality.

PRUFROCK: Once again, bears were unleashed against forces that really had no idea how to deal with them. They moved fast over difficult ground, they lived off the land, sometimes off the people - there were stories from this time of Bears eating Swedish villagers - they completely unstrung enemy cavalry. Working in numbers, they were unstoppable

By 1455 the Swedes had enough, only Charles II wanted to keep fighting. Within a year, by 1456, a nobleman named Erik Axelson Tott, and the Swedish Archbishop Jons Bengtsson, organized the overthrow of Charles II and a surrender to Christian. The Kalmar Union was back.

However, the unified Kalmar state of 1456, was, if anything even more fractious. Sweden had been beaten and humiliated, it was left subjugated and resentful. Within a decade, the Swedes, led by Tott and Bengtsson revolted, and Charles II returned with a force of German and Polish mercenaries in 1467.

Again, the Bear Cavalry were recalled to battle in 1468, but if anything this only increased Swedish resistance.

Charles II was beheaded on the field of battle by the great bear Wotan in 1472, and Swedish resistance subsided, but did not vanish.

Guerilla warfare took a toll on bears, by 1474, the last of the Bear Cavalry; their numbers extremely depleted, were withdrawn and went home. Low level actions and resistance continued up to 1477, when Christian was forced to compromise on self government with Swedish nobility.

The Swedish conflict essentially froze Danish involvement in Germany and the rest of Europe, and bankrupted the treasury. The attention of the Kalmar Union was entirely internal. At a critical period of time, the Kalmar Union, and the Danish kingdom, were on the sidelines. The victories of Christian I would not last, if anything, the Swedes were even more committed to their independence.

Christian I was succeeded by his son John, who took power in Norway and Denmark in 1483. Sweden failed to elect him king, and continued with the regent Sten Stur until 1496, until John conquered the land in a short, sharp war - again, the Bear Cavalry was deployed.

A few years later, the Bear Cavalry were brought to bear on Germany in a war over Schleswig Holstein in 1500, but although the bears did well, John did not.

Encouraged by this failure, Sweden again went its own way in 1505. John died in a fall from a horse in 1513.

John's son Christian II took over, ruling from 1513 to 1523. Christian's priority was to bring Sweden back into the Union, by force if necessary. An early believer in total warfare, Christian II deployed Bear Cavalry immediately beginning in 1518. It would be the last major action by the Bear Cavalry in large numbers.

By 1520 Sweden was conquered once again, but within three years, Christian's harsh rule had brought about his downfall. Gustav Vasa broke away in Sweden, and Christian II was in Denmark and Norway replaced by Frederick.

Frederick's rule lasted ten years, until 1533, and he spent most of it fighting internal revolts and efforts by Christian II's supporters to return him to the throne. The Bear Cavalry, seen as loyal to Christian II was left in Iceland.

Christian III, replaced Frederick in 1533, and remained in power until 1559. During this time, Christian fought several revolts within Denmark itself. Like Christian II, he called for Bear Cavalry almost immediately in 1533.

By this time, however, the deployment of Bear Cavalry had become extremely expensive. With military success, the price had gone up, the Icelanders were less and less willing to simply cross the seas for glory. And it had gotten more dangerous, every time the Bear Cavalry had been used, casualties had gone up. People, particularly swedes, were getting better and better at coping with bears... particularly in guerilla actions.

Less than a few hundred bears crossed over to join Christian III in his battles against internal revolt. These bears were let loose on civilian populations, quickly establishing a reputation for terror and brutality.

Public support or tolerance of the Bear Cavalry, even by Christian III's supporters declined rapidly. By 1535, the last of the bears and their riders had been sent home. Christian III considered the deployment of Bear Cavalry against his own people as one of his great mistakes. After that, he avoided getting involved in wars.

It was just about the end for Bear Cavalry. They would be involved in only two more battles, a generation later, in 1559 and 1563.

****

THE NEXT SCENE is a quiet scene set in a green room. There's a large square coffee table filled with snacks and drinks, and two couches. PRUFROCK sits on one of the couches. Two young film makers, BJORK KARASAN and her partner BRAGI GRONDEL, sit on the other. The camera is stationary, except for occasional close ups. Subtitles flash, showing their names, with the subheading 'local film makers.'

PRUFROCK (VOICE OVER): While we were shooting the documentary, we came across a couple of local film makers, trying to raise money for their own movie.

PRUFROCK: So this isn't a documentary.

BRAGI GRONDEL: (heavily accented): No, it's an epic. It's about the saga of Wotan.

PRUFROCK: Wotan is a fighting bear from the reign of Christian I?

BJORK KARASAN: Yes... and no. Wotan was part of the bear Cavalry, he and his rider Sigur. He was the biggest fighting bear ever. He stood ten feet tall.

BRAGI GRONDEL: Eleven.

BJORK KARASAN: Eleven! He was unstoppable in battle! He was the one who beheaded Charles of Sweden, one swipe! The war is over. There are all these stories of his strength. It's an adventure, it's an epic.

BRAGI GRONDEL: It's a story about love. There's tragedy. There was a battle, and Sigur was killed, and Wotan went Berserk.

BJORK KARASAN: Totally berserk

CLOSE UP OF PRUFROCK LISTENING INTENTLY.

BRAGI GRONDEL: Just insane... with grief, you see. And that's it, the battle was over. Wotan's anger shook the mountains. Everyone who could fled. Both armies, they fled.

BJORK KARASAN: But some couldn't. Yes, and of those left, both sides were forced to come together, to join together to fight or escape Wotan. It's this huge battle all over again.

BRAGI GRONDEL: And nothing can stop Wotan, but his own grief. Finally, he goes to where Sigur has fallen and lays down.

BJORK KARASAN: And dies.

BRAGI GRONDEL: The end, roll credits.

CLOSE UP OF BRAGI GRONDEL, LOOKING PASSIONATE, A TEAR FORMING IN THE CORNER OF ONE EYE.

PRUFROCK: Okay, so what do you need from me?

BRAGI GRONDEL: Well, we're trying to raise money for the film, so it would be good if you could mention us.... You know, that we are working on this project... I know you've got your own movie. But we really respect your work.

PRUFROCK NODS.

BJORK KARASAN: It's tough to get a movie made.

PRUFROCK: Why do you want to get this movie made?

BJORK KARASAN: Iceland is boring! We've got nothing really. Some rocks, some glaciers, nothing ever happened here. Really, without the Bear Cavalry.... that's our big thing, that's the one thing we are really known for, that puts us on the map.... Without the bears, there's nothing special...

****

The Bear Cavalry — Page 118

CUT TO PRUFROCK SITTING ON A ROCK IN THE ICELANDIC COUNTRYSIDE, CAMERA PANS ACROSS THE SCENERY, AUSTERE AND MAGNIFICENT.

PRUFROCK VOICE OVER: What could I say? I promised to see what I could do for them.

CAMERA CONTINUES PANNING ACROSS THE VAST ICELANDIC LANDSCAPE, SLOWLY FOCUSES IN ON PRUFROCK, SITTING ON A BOULDER, OVERLOOKING A GLACIER.

PRUFROCK: One of the things I've really enjoyed about this documentary series, about this documentary is the chance to go places, to meet people, to see the interesting things we get up to, the amazing things people do, amazing people, amazing places.

PAUSES

PRUFROCK: The thing is, I don't think I've ever met anyone who wasn't interesting, I've never been any place that wasn't amazing. The whole world, everything in it, is wonderful and special, and I've never seen anyone or anything that was really boring. We're talking about bears, and it was really nice to meet these film makers and try to help them out with their movie, good luck guys.

PAUSES

PRUFROCK: But I think they got it wrong when they said that's all there is to Iceland. It's an amazing place, amazing people. I think that everything is amazing if you look at it right.

****

NEW SEQUENCE. MONTAGE OF IMAGES - PULP MAGAZINES, WORKS OF ART, MOVIE CLIPS,

TEDDY ROOSEVELT RIDING THE GRIZZLY UP SAN JUAN HILL.

PRUFROCK VOICE OVER: They are right about one thing. The Bear Cavalry captured the world's imagination. After 1563, the last actual use of bears in war, the bear cavalry was the subject of over 800 works of art in the remainder of the 16th century alone.

Shakespeare alluded to it in several of his plays.

Ben Johnson, Shakespeare's contemporary actually wrote a play about it. They got actors in costumes to play the bears. It didn't go over well, apparently, Elizabethan audiences demanded real bears. Apparently it was Johnson's greatest flop.

The Elizabethan Bear Gardens, which was actually a pretty awful and sadistic form of entertainment, also traded on the notoriety of the bear cavalry, with attendants dressing in cavalry costume.

Bear cavalry, either individual, or in battle scenes were a favorite of renaissance painters, and throughout Italy, you can actually find churches depicting scenes of bears on their walls.

IMAGE: STATIONS OF THE CROSS, WITH THE ROMANS RIDING BEARS. A REARING ANGRY BEAR DEFENDING CHRIST FROM THE PHARISEES. WAR BEARS PROSTRATING THEMSELVES AT JESUS' FEET WHILE FRUSTRATED ROMAN SOLDIERS LOOK ON. JESUS AND MARY MAGDALEN SHARING AN APPLE WHILE RIDING SIDE-SADDLE.

PRUFROCK VOICE OVER: Cosimo de Medici....

CUT TO A PORTRAIT OF A LONG NOSED RENAISSANCE PATRIARCH

PRUFROCK VOICE OVER: caused a sensation when he rode an Icelandic bear through the streets of Milan.

CRUDE WOODCUT OF MEDICI AND THE BEAR.

PRUFROCK VOICE OVER: ...which lead to a short lived fad that ended rather badly.

RENAISSANCE PAINTING OF A BEAR DRAGGING DOWN ITS NOBLEMAN RIDER AND TEARING HIM APART, THE NOBLEMAN SCREAMING, AS THE CROWD LOOKS ON IN SHOCK AND HORROR.

PRUFROCK VOICE OVER: It became one of the staples of Renaissance art.

MARBLE STATUE OF GENERAL GAULTHERIA OF FLORENCE, MOUNTED ON A REARING BEAR, THE ANIMAL'S JAWS GAPING, FOREPAW CLAWING THE AIR, ONE OF MICHAELANGELO'S MOST FAMOUS WORKS.

PRUFROCK VOICE OVER: He never rode that by the way, completely made up.

Through the 17th and 18th century the momentum simply picked up. Bears were a regular subject of woodcuts, artwork. Sometimes subject matter, sometimes inserted.

A PASTORAL SCENE OF CHILDREN AT PLAY, CAMERA ZOOMS INTO THE RIGHT HAND CORNER OF THE PICTURE, WHERE A SQUAD OF SOLDIERS ON BEARS CAN BE SEEN, THEIR OFFICER TURNING TO GESTURE AS HE LEADS THEM.

PRUFROCK VOICE OVER: The Emperor of China himself, when receiving westerners, wanted to know about the bear cavalry.

ORIENTAL PAINTING OF THE EMPEROR IN COURT, STROKING HIS CHIN, AS HIS ADVISORS COUNSEL HIM. NO BEARS VISIBLE.

PRUFROCK VOICE OVER: Bear riders and cavalry appeared in poems by Shelly and Keats. Lord Byron tried to ride one, resulting in his injuries.

HOGARTH'S CHARCOAL - BYRON AND THE BEAR.

PRUFROCK VOICE OVER: Alexander Dumas had one of his Musketeers, Porthos, riding an Icelandic bear.

A COLOURED ARTISTS ILLUSTRATION FROM THE NOVEL, D'ARTAGNAN ON HIS HORSE, AND PORTHOS ON HIS BEAR.

PRUFROCK VOICE OVER: For some reason, this phenomenon caught something in the western imagination, and continued to have a life of its own long after the actual bear cavalry was an obsolete footnote.

****

PRUFROCK IN A CRAMPED ARTISTS STUDIO. THE STUDIO IS FILLED TO THE BRIM WITH PAINTINGS, MOSTLY IN RENAISSANCE STYLE, IN VARIOUS STAGES OF COMPLETIN, ALONG WITH SKETCHES, STUDIES, REFERENCE BOOKS, PAINTS, BRUSHES, SKETCH PADS AND AN EASEL. PRUFROCK IS TALKING TO A MAN WOMAN, THE ARTIST.

PRUFROCK VOICE OVER: This is BJORN-SANDERSON, a prominent 'Bear Artist.'

BJORN SANDERSON: (Smiles) Actually I prefer to think of myself as primarily Renaissance style. I just like the look and feel of it, the way they handle light, the compositions. I do

The Bear Cavalry – Page 122

other styles, other eras from time to time. Modernism, pointillism. I like the Flemish masters.

PRUFROCK: Bears show up in a lot of your paintings though.

BJORN SANDERSON: Well yes (laughs). Bears play a big part in iconography. Bears and horses.

PRUFROCK: Why do you use Bears so prominently?

MONTAGE OF BJORN SANDERSON PAINTINGS, VERSIONS OF ZEUS DEVOURING IT'S CHILDREN, BUT WITH BEAR AS ZEUS, STUDIES OF RENAISSANCE WILDLIFE, CONDOTTIERI MERCENARIES RIDING BEARS, COPIES OF WELL KNOWN RENAISSANCE PAINTINGS WITH BEARS IN THE ROLE OF GODS AND MONSTERS, GREEK SCENES, SOCRATES LECTURING BEARS, JULIUS CAESAR, NAPOLEON ASTRIDE BEARS.

BJORN SANDERSON (VOICE OVER): Bears are an interesting subject, because they can walk upright. So they straddle that boundary between human and animal, so that makes them a natural subject for anything that deals with the supernatural, when you're depicting gods and monsters. They don't fit as angels or devils, they're avatars of chaos, of nature, of supernatural power that can be either friendly or benign. They represented nature, and the new world. They were a major metaphor in Enlightenment thinking, you find Rousseau referring to them constantly. Locke, Voltaire, even Benjamin Franklin; wrote about bears, using them to make some point about natural law or history or economics.

FOOTAGE OF BJORN SANDERSON AT HIS EASEL, SKETCHING A CHARCOAL STUDY, A PICTURE OF NAPOLEAN CROSSING THE ALPS AS A

REFERENCE, SHOWING NAPOLEON ON A REARING BEAR.

BJORN SANDERSON (TALKING TO PRUFROCK): The other part is this medieval history of the Bear Cavalry in Scandinavia. They were active for such a short time, but they left an indelible impression in history. You can ride them. They represent power and ferocity, but you can ride them like a horse, and that's powerful, even iconic.

CUT TO MORE PAINTINGS AND SKETCHES.

BJORN SANDERSON (VOICE OVER): I like bears, they're fun to draw, and they liven up almost any subject.

CUT TO ACTUAL HISTORICAL PAINTINGS AND SCULPTURE AND MUSEUM. AND WARHOL'S 'STUDIES IN GRIZZLY.' POP ART BEARS. YOGI AND BOO BOO.

BJORN SANDERSON: Voice over. People have been using bears in art since Shakespeare's time. It's a recurrent theme. I'm known for it, but I'm hardly the first and I won't be the last. They're simply embedded in pop culture. They're not going to go away any time soon.

****

REYJAVIK ICELAND, NATIONAL MUSEUM, BEAR GALLERY.

PRUFROCK AND PROFESSOR HUGO ARNHEIM ARE WANDERING THROUGH THE GALLERY. THE GALLERY IS FULL OF MEDIEVAL WEAPONS, STATUES OF BEARS AND RIDERS IN ARMOUR, SOME OF IT QUITE DENTED, PAINTINGS ON THE WALLS SHOWING SCENES OF THE BATTLES.

PRUFROCK: So what happened to the Bear Cavalry? What was their undoing? Firearms?

HUGO ARNHEIM: Well, yes and no. Arquebus's had been used since the 14th century, through the entire period of Bear Cavalry. But they were a low velocity firearm, so plate armor provided some protection. (pause) Indeed, one of the ways they used to test plate armor was to fire an Arquebus at it.

PRUFROCK: Cool!

QUICK SHOT OF A BREASTPLATE WITH A GAPING HOLE THROUGH IT. PRUFROCK STICKS HIS FINGERS THROUGH THE HOLE, AND LOOKS AT ARNHEIM.

HUGO ARNHEIM: It didn't always work.

PRUFROCK: Okay, so it's 1559. What's happening?

HUGO ARNHEIM: Frederick II comes to power in Denmark.

CUT TO PORTRAIT OF FREDERICK II.

HUGO ARNHEIM: Now, by this time, the Kalmar Union is over. 1523, Gustav Vasa is the King of Sweden, he takes it out of the Union. Denmark and Sweden fight it out, but the Danes can't hold it.

Still, in late medieval terms, this is pretty fresh. Literally, it's only a generation or two ago. In some of these places, they're fighting wars over claims that date back centuries.

Now, Frederick II, he is a modernist Prince. He's a typical renaissance man of his era, interested in arts and letters, very involved in governance, and very much a child of his time, a prince of his time.

PRUFROCK: By which you mean he was all about conquering his neighbors.

ARNHEIM (chuckles): Not quite. Although in 1559, one of his first acts was conquering the Dithmarschen.

PRUFROCK (Looks confused): Dit-Martians?

HUGO ARNHEIM: Dithmarschen.

QUICK CUT TO A MAP, SHOWING DITHMARSCHEN AS A SMALL PROVINCE IN THE SOUTH OF DENMARK, JUST OFF OF SCHLESWIG HOLSTEIN.

PRUFROCK: This was one of the last battles of the Bear Cavalry?

HUGO ARNHEIM: The last successful battle, actually. The Dithmarschen was a peasant army, they were a Peasants Republic basically trying to preserve their independence.

Frederick appointed Count Johann Rantzau from Stenburg to carry on the campaign.

Count Rantzau was not exactly a fan of Bear Cavalry. His traditions were German. But Frederick was insisting, and they were available. Rantzau used the tools that he had available.

The conditions were optimal. We had a highly organized Bear Cavalry just cutting through what amounted to a poorly organized peasant militia. The campaign was over very quickly, the peasants surrendered, and Rantzau was impressed. He actually wrote a monograph about it.

CUT TO - PORTRAIT OF THE BATTLEFIELD. A VOICE READS FROM RANTZAU'S LETTER.

VOICE OVER: In respect of the Bears, I was much surprised by their discipline and order, particularly given the natural state of savagery of such beasts as we witnessed on the field of battle. This, I feel, is the true lesson. Valor and savagery are the illusions of virtue - useful on the battlefield, but everywhere else a disaster, and the battle is only the tiniest though most vital portion of an army's work. Thus mettle in battle alone is useless as with no other steel, such mettle will rapidly unmake an army long before the battle. The lesson to be taken from the Bears is not their passion, but their forbearance. Discipline and order was their advantage, even more than their ferocity. This discipline and order was absent among the peasants. This, I feel is the key...

PRUFROCK: So what happens next?

HUGO ARNHEIM: Well, in 1563, the Northern Seven Years War breaks out. This represents Frederick's effort to re-establish the Kalmar Union. Sweden was then ruled by his cousin, King Erik the fourteenth who was mad...

PRUFROCK: By mad you mean...?

HUGO ARNHEIM: How do you say it ... A few sandwiches short of a picnic? His elevator only reached alternate floors? Mad. Loony toons. Schizophrenic, perhaps manic depressive.

CUT TO PORTRAIT OF ERIK XIV, A REDHEADED MAN WITH A LONG NARROW BEARD DIVIDED INTO FORKS.

PRUFROCK: As if we couldn't tell from his facial hair.

HUGO ARNHEIM: Yes, well like all monarchs, Erik was also ambitious. He wanted to make Sweden a great power, he was trying to expand into the Baltic. His interests clashed with Charles and the war was on...

In August and September, the Danes marched into Sweden, with fighting at Alvsborg and Halmstad. The Swedes were beaten back. The Bear Cavalry was at the forefront of these campaigns, and took heavy losses, even though the Danes won.

PRUFROCK: And that was the last battle?

ARNHEIM: The last battle anyone talks about. There was one more....

****

CLOSE UP OF A STUFFED SNARLING BEAR, FANGS GLISTENING, COVERED WITH ARMOUR, REARING OVER A COUPLE OF TERRIFIED PEASANT SOLDIERS.

CUT TO THE FIELDS OF AXTORNA, SWEDEN. ARNHEIM AND PRUFROCK ARE STANDING ON THIS BATTLEFIELD, A HILLSIDE STREWN WITH STONES.

HUGO ARNHEIM: The war, on land at least, consistently went in Denmark's favor. Denmark was fielding an army of professional mercenaries, by nature highly trained, and highly disciplined. The Swedish force was composed of peasant levies, poorly trained and disciplined recruits. So normally, the Danes cut the Swedes to pieces.

It's lucky for the Swedes that the Mercenary Army is so expensive that Frederick can only use it to partial effect. They keep waiting for the check to clear. There are only two areas where the Swedes are particularly successful....

PRUFROCK: Those are...

HUGO ARNHEIM: The navy. You can't run a navy with peasant levies. A certain amount of professionalism and inherent skill and discipline is required. The Swedish navy consistently beat the Danish navy.

PRUFROCK: And the other?

HUGO ARNHEIM: Shooting bears.

CUT TO: GRAPHIC IMAGE OF AN ARMOURED WAR BEAR REARING UP - SUDDENLY IN THE CENTRE OF THE BEAR, A BIG RED BULLS EYE WITH CROSS HAIRS APPEARS. THEN SMALLER CROSS HAIRS JUST ABOVE THAT. THEN A PROLIFERATION OF BULLS EYES AND CROSS HAIRS ALL OVER THE BEAR'S HEAD AND TORSO.

CUT BACK TO ARNHEIM AND PRUFROCK CLAMBERING OVER THE BATTLEFIELD, THEY'RE TOO FAR AWAY FOR A BOOM MIKE, THEIR VOICES DUBBED OVER.

HUGO ARNHEIM VOICE OVER: In Iceland, Axtorna is remembered as the 'Battle from Which No One Came Back. At Alvsborg and Halmstad, the casualty rates for Bear Cavalry were high. 40 per cent, and 48 per cent respectively. At Axtorna mortality was 95 per cent.

PRUFROCK VOICE OVER: What happened?

HUGO ARNHEIM VOICE OVER: You have to remember the history of the bear cavalry in Sweden. It wasn't like now, with that veneer of romance and the exotic.

To the Swedes, the bear cavalry was absolutely nightmarish. An unstoppable force in battle, and even worse, loosed on towns and villages they were horrific, eating people, tearing children limb from limb.

They were utterly terrifying. After two generations, they had elevated to full grown nightmares. It was like Satan himself entering the battlefield.

PRUFROCK VOICE OVER: So they got attention.

The Bear Cavalry – Page 129

HUGO ARNHEIM VOICE OVER: Indeed. And they attracted a lot of firepower. Anyone with an Arquebus among the Swedes was aiming at the bears. Bears killed at Halmstad, it was found, had an average of a dozen bullets in them. People kept firing at the animals even after they were down.

PRUFROCK VOICE OVER: Awesome. And between Halmstad and Axtorna? Why did the mortality climb so much?

HUGO ARNHEIM VOICE OVER: Ahhh, that was a revolution!

CUT BACK TO THE MUSEUM - HALL OF WEAPONS. ARNHEIM IS HOLDING UP AN ARQUEBUS AND SHOWING IT TO PRUFROCK.

HUGO ARNHEIM: Now, up to this time, Arquebus' had been loaded and fired pretty much on an individual basis. So firing was sporadic, people aimed, and hit or missed, mostly missed. Axtorna is the first instance of concentrated disciplined fire. They were all firing at the same targets, or the same areas.

Essentially, at Axtorna, the Arquebus men were organized together, and more than that, they broke into three groups - each group fired in unison, stepped back for the second group, reloaded, and were ready to step forward and fire again, after the third group. That way they could put a rotating sustained concentrated fire.

PRUFROCK: Like a human machine gun?

HUGO ARNHEIM: Yes! It devastated the Bear Cavalry, they were too big, too tempting a target. The Swedes were terrified of bears, so that's where they aimed. It devastated the Danish soldiers too although the Swedes came very close to losing that battle. It was a revolution in the use of firearms, and that lesson filtered through the Swedish army.

PRUFROCK: And that was it for bears?

HUGO ARNHEIM: Yes, many of the Bear Cavalry had been extremely discouraged by the outcomes at Alvsborg and Halmstad. The almost total losses of Axtorna broke their spirits utterly. The Danish Commander, Rantzau, who came from a German background had never been entirely comfortable with the Bear Cavalry, a lot of officers still considered it a Carnival sideshow. So they took the opportunity to retire it.

PRUFROCK: The Bears went home?

HUGO ARNHEIM: Yes. The Bears went home, or were put to death, or sold off to Bear gardens, or eccentric nobles. Many of the officers and men in the bear Cavalry were reassigned to regular cavalry, artillery or other divisions. The lucky few riders made it back to Iceland. No bears made it back.

PRUFROCK: And that was it?

HUGO ARNHEIM: The last use of Bears in war? Yes. Although for ceremonial reasons, the Danish Kings maintained an Icelandic Bear guard, and they would be used for parades, special occasions, show off - but that was really akin to a military band, not a fighting force.

PRUFROCK: And that's the end of the story?

HUGO ARNHEIM: In a sense. Of course, nothing really ends. The fall of the bear cavalry produced revolutions in military organization in both Denmark and Sweden.

The War dragged on until about 1570 when both sides were too exhausted to keep fighting. The results were inconclusive.

The Bear Cavalry – Page 131

No one got what they wanted. But Sweden ended up with a standing army, and developed a new set of tactics around the use of Arquebus volleys, tactics that would not be used elsewhere in Europe for a generation or more.

This was the beginning of a Swedish Imperial phase in which they punched far above their weight, fought wars with Russia and established an Empire around the Baltic. Their early lead was literally game changing.

PRUFROCK: And Denmark?

HUGO ARNHEIM: Denmark was slower to adopt Arquebus volleys. Not as slow as the rest of Europe. But the discipline required for a Bear Cavalry had been noted and appreciated; the reassignments of the personnel assigned to the Cavalry produced a wave of reform, making the Danish Army the single most professional fighting force in Europe. Denmark proceeded to become a dominant power in Germany almost right up to the Revolutionary war period.

PRUFROCK: Denmark and Norway, did they ever have a rematch?

HUGO ARNHEIM: Oh god no. Those two nations never fought again, they both channeled their imperial ambitions in completely different directions.

****

OPENING SCENE - ASBRINGNNASTAT FESTIVAL PEOPLE WALKING BACK AND FORTH IN THE BACKGROUND, BEAR SHAPED HELIUM BALLOONS, TOURISTS. IN THE FOREGROUND, PRUFROCK, WEARING BRIGHT RED PLASTIC ARMOUR. WITH HIM ARE TWO OTHER MEN, JON AND ARN, BOTH WEARING THE SAME ARMOUR,

The Bear Cavalry – Page 132

ONE WITH WHAT LOOKS LIKE A GRAY
BASKETBALL UNDER HIS ARM.

PRUFROCK: Welcome back to the Asbringnnastat. We've
had all the races, the events. We're coming up to the big one.
What's this called?

JON: (leaning forward, grinning) Stridsvartabirni.

PRUFROCK TRIES TO PRONOUNCE IT A FEW
TIMES, BEING CORRECT.

PRUFROCK: (laughing) What he said. So what is it exactly?

ARN: The Stridsvartabirni is the war of the bears. We have ....
teams, you see. Men riding bears. And each time, of men and
bears, they try to get the ball.

JON: It is like hockey.

ARN: Hockey But with bears.

PRUFROCK: So like Polo, but bears instead of horses.

JON: Yes. But not with sticks, the bears smash the ball
themselves.

ARN: It started back in the 15th century, preparing for battle.
Now, we do it for fun.

PRUFROCK: Cool. So there are matches between
enthusiasts all year, and it breaks down into four main teams,
who fight it out at the Asbringnnastat. This year, I've been
invited to ride with the Red team.

ARN (Grins and gives thumbs up): Robin! He is our man!

PRUFROCK: How could I turn this down? I have to wonder
about all this body armor.

JON: Oh that's just so you aren't killed while playing.

PRUFROCK: Killed?

ARN (laughing): Oh, don't worry. It is safe as houses.

JON: Yes, don't worry. We will look after you.

ARN: Robin! In honor of your movie we have a present for you.

JON: Yes, the ball. Tradition is that we call the ball Olaf, and we paint a face on it.

ARN: (holding up the ball, and turning it around to face the camera. The face on the ball sports ROBIN PRUFROCK's handlebar mustache).

PRUFROCK: doubles over with laughter, shakes their hands.

PRUFROCK VOICE OVER: Of course, before I could participate in a rousing game of Bear Polo, I had to learn to ride a bear.

MONTAGE OF CLIPS - ROBIN PRUFROCK LEARNING TO RIDE A BEAR. PETTING ONE. CLIMBING ON. SITTING UNEASILY WHILE ONE IS BEING LEAD AROUND IN A CIRCLE, THE CAMERA PULLS BACK TO SHOW THAT ROBIN IS THE ONLY ADULT ON A BEAR. HE IS WITH A GROUP OF CHILDREN LEARNING ON TAME BEARS. MORE CLIPS.

PRUFROCK AND HELGA HAPLARSON, WITH A PLACID RED FURRED BEAR, WHO IS, FOR SOME REASON, WEARING A PORKPIE HAT WITH FLOWERS STICKING OUT OF IT. THE BEAR'S NAME IS GERTA. HELGA IS TEACHING PRUFROCK TO SADDLE A BEAR.

HELGA HAPLARSON: Now, Robin, this is important you put the saddle back just before the hips. Is not a horse, all your comic books, they are wrong. Bear is not like a horse, the saddle in the middle of the back is too much weight there.

DEMONSTRATES THE PLACEMENT OF THE SADDLE. PRUFROCK NODS.

HELGA HAPLARSON: Uncomfortable for the bear. He will get angry and kill you. Also, when he rears up, you will fall off. Very silly.

PRUFROCK: Wait? What was that last part?

HELGA HAPLARSON: You will fall off.

PRUFROCK: I meant the part about being killed.

HELGA HAPLARSON (laughs): Oh do not worry about that. Just make sure that the saddle rides towards the back, just ahead of their hips. Simple!

PRUFROCK: I will make sure to remember that.

HELGA HAPLARSON: Now, pay close attention, I will show you how to cinch the straps.

PRUFROCK (attentive): Okay.

HELGA HAPLARSON: Good, now this way and this way. Never that way. If you get them crossed, or backwards, bear will not be comfortable. He will kill you. But do not worry, I will teach you a little nursery rhyme my mother taught me, and you will not forget to do it right.

PRUFROCK (dubious): All right.

HELGA HAPLARSON: Also, this strap here, by the bear's private parts. Not too loose, but not too tight. Or...

PRUFROCK: Or the bear will get angry and kill me?

HELGA HAPLARSON: Oh no He will get very very angry. You will wish he just killed you. But do not worry, it is easy, once you have the trick. It is like this....

HELGA GUIDES PRUFROCK'S HAND ALONG THE STRAPS. THE BEAR, GERTA, GROWLS LOUDLY. PRUFROCK BACKS OFF SEVERAL FEET.

HELGA SLAPS GERTA ON THE MUZZLE AND SAYS SOMETHING IN ICELANDIC. GERTA HANGS ITS HEAD.

HELGA HAPLARSON: She's never like that!

PRUFROCK VOICE OVER: I decided to leave this part to the professionals.

ROBIN FALLING OFF BEARS REPEATEDLY. CLOSE UPS ON THE BEARS EXPRESSIONS. PEOPLE HELPING PRUFROCK BACK.

CUT TO EDITING SUITE, PAUL BJORNSON AND PRUFROCK.

PAUL BJORNSON: How many shots of you falling off a bear do we need?

PRUFROCK: My son thinks they're hilarious.

PAUL BJORNSON: Your son is eight years old, and he can't tell the difference between an axe murderer and a fireman.

PRUFROCK: He can too! Firemen have red hats!

PAUL BJORNSON: I'm just saying we should tighten it up a little bit. You know, for the parts of the audience that aren't eight years old.

PRUFROCK: All right.

CUT TO MONTAGE OF LEARNING TO MOUNT UP. PRUFROCK APPROACHING BEARS WITH INCREASING CONFIDENCE. TWO OR THREE PEOPLE ASSISTING AND DEMONSTRATING. CLIMBING ON WITH INCREASING CONFIDENCE. FALLING OFF.

PRUFROCK VOICE OVER: I had the help of the team members who coached me through it. They really went out of their way. It was an exhilarating, sometimes terrifying experience.

SHIFT TO MONTAGE ON PRUFROCK ON BEARS, THE BEAR BEING LEAD BY HANDLERS. SLOWLY TAKING THE REINS AND GUIDING THE BEAR. SOMETIMES THE BEAR GOING WHERE IT WANTED AS PRUFROCK LOOKS HAPLESSLY AT THE CAMERA. SOMETIMES FALLING OFF, BUT MOUNTING BACK UP AGAIN.

PRUFROCK VOICE OVER: I got the hang of it.

ROBIN ON A GALLOPING BEAR, WHOOPING WITH EXHILARATION.

EVENTUALLY A CLOSING SHOT OF ROBIN IN A COWBOY HAT, AMBLING ALONG, THE CAMERA PULLS BACK FAR ENOUGH TO SEE ROBIN ON A BEAR, WALKING OFF INTO THE SUNSET AS HE WAVES HIS HAT.

****

MONTAGE OF STUFFED BEARS, BEAR FIGURINES, BEAR SIGNS. FOLLOWED BY SCENES OF REGULAR PEOPLE GOING ABOUT THEIR BUSINESS IN ICELAND.

The Bear Cavalry — Page 137

PRUFROCK VOICE OVER: Icelanders are people just like everywhere else. They get up in the morning, they have breakfast. they go to work, they go to movies, they relax, have families. In a sense, people are just people the world over.

But it's amazing how 'Bear' influenced the Icelandic culture is. Everywhere you go, you see it. It's a defining thing. I suppose it's like cowboys in the west. Everyone's wearing a cowboy hat. Hear, although most people can live their whole life without riding a bear, or going to a bear farm, it's very much their thing.

And some people actually get right into it.

CAMERA OPENS ON PRUFROCK IN A VAST WAREHOUSE. A MATRONLY MIDDLE AGED WOMAN IS WITH HIM.

PRUFROCK: This is backstage at something that translates as the Bear Show. I'm here with Helga Haplarson.

HELGA HAPLARSON: Hello.

PRUFROCK: Tell us about this part. What is going on here?

AS THEY WALK THROUGH THE BUILDING IT BECOMES APPARENT THAT IT IS A BEAR STABLE. DIFFERENT BEARS ARE IN PENS, WATCHING THEM GO BY.

HELGA HAPLARSON (thickly accented and struggling with English): Well... this is the bear showing. It is like a dog show, you know, like in the pictures. People raise up their bears, some breed them. Sometimes farm bears, sometimes just in the family, some lines have been in a family for ten generations.

PRUFROCK: So people bring their bears, and it's for show. They don't do anything? They don't race, they don't kick a basketball.

HELGA HAPLARSON: No, it's .... we look for appearance, coat, quality of fur, posture... behaviour.... like that.

PRUFROCK: Okay.

HELGA HAPLARSON: And we like to dress them up.

PRUFROCK: What?

HELGA HAPLARSON: We dress them up.

QUICK CUT TO A CHIHUAHUA IN A RIDICULOUS COSTUME.

PRUFROCK: In clothes?

HELGA HAPLARSON: Yes, clothes sometimes. Sometimes in armor. Especially, armor from the wars, very valuable, very impressive. Not everyone can do that. Sometimes costumes, like an astronaut or a fireman, or like James Bond.

QUICK CUT TO - ROBIN'S FACE, ABSOLUTELY AMAZED AND INCREDULOUS. THEN CUT TO A MONTAGE OF TOY DOGS, MINIATURES DRESSED UP IN VARIOUS COSTUMES.

PRUFROCK: And the bears put up with this?

HELGA HAPLARSON: Oh yes, (enthusiastically) they love it!

PRUFROCK: Uh huh (sounding doubtful)

HELGA HAPLARSON: Of course, there are all sorts of categories.

AS THEY TALK THEY'VE BEEN WALKING ALONG PAST THE STALLS. PRUFROCK COMES TO A STOP.

PRUFROCK: My god! That one's huge. He's like an SUV with Fur.

HELGA REACHES IN TO TOUSLE ITS HEAD.

HELGA HAPLARSON: This is my darling, this is Stig. He is the biggest.... How you say.. a record setter. He doesn't compete. He is almost as big as Wotan. You know about Wotan?

PRUFROCK: Yes, I've heard about him.

HELGA HAPLARSON (almost bubbling with excitement): We have a special event this year. This year.... We have a loan from the museum. Special permission, it was approved in Cabinet! Stig will wear Wotan's armor. The first time it has been worn in 500 years.

PRUFROCK: As long as it's safe....

HELGA HAPLARSON: Oh, yes, yes... Safe! Completely safe!

CUT TO A FIVE MINUTE SEQUENCE OF THE BEAR SHOWS - BEARS PARADING PAST IN ARMOUR, SOME WITH ARMOURED RIDERS, SOME REARING UP TO SHOW OFF THE ARMOUR.

THEN THE 'IMAGINATIVE' SECTION - PLASTIC ARMOUR, ASTRONAUTS, FANTASY OR SCIENCE FICTION THEMES, A HEAVY METAL ROCK STAR, A STRANGE WRAPAROUND COSTUME OF LIGHTS AND TUBING.

ONE DRESSED AS A FIREMAN. ANOTHER AS AN EXPLORER. A SOLDIER.

OCCASIONAL CUTS TO AN APPRECIATIVE
AUDIENCE

As the sequence plays HELGA'S voice is heard -

HELGA HAPLARSON VOICE OVER: My family has been
bear breeders for a long time. My great grandfather began.
There are not that many of us, but we perform a valuable
service. We maintain the breeds and bloodlines.

PAN OVER THE STALLS, COMING TO REST ON
HELGA RUBBING STIG'S IMMENSE HEAD.

HELGA HAPLARSON VOICE OVER: I know Stig's
ancestors better than my own. He is a sweet boy.

****

CUT TO SHOT OF ROBIN PRUFROCK SITTING IN A
CHAIR. HE STARES AT THE CAMERA. HE LOOKS
VERY SERIOUS.

PRUFROCK: Okay, we'll have cautions at the beginning of
the documentary, and at the end, but I just wanted to say this
officially, right there. I know that we may have a lot of
children watching this documentary. I know that we may
have some people watching who may feel reckless, or have
poor judgement, or who may remember this when they're
under the influence and not as careful as they should be.

PAUSE

PRUFROCK: In this documentary, we learn a lot about
bears, and we actually see people interacting with tame or
domesticated bears, we see bear riders, people at festivals,
even people playing sports with them. I need to say this:

Don't do that! Bears, even domesticated ones, are powerful
dangerous animals. They can hurt or kill you, without even

The Bear Cavalry — Page 141

meaning to. And they can lash out if you handle them wrong. The people we've met who farm bears, who handle them, who ride them or play games with them, they're experienced. You aren't.

Don't take chances. If you're in Iceland, or dealing with tame or domesticated Icelandic bears, leave them alone. Leave them to the people who know how to handle them.

And for God's sakes, never approach a wild bear under any circumstances. Not any kind of wild bear. Always treat them with respect, give them distance, and be careful. They are incredibly dangerous.

I don't want anyone to get hurt or killed because they saw this documentary and made a mistake.

So remember, be careful.

****

STRIDSVARTABIRNI!!!

OPENING SHOT - ON THE PLAYING FIELD. RIDERS ARE WALKING AROUND WITH THEIR BEARS. THEY WEAR ELABORATE PLASTIC ARMOUR, WITH HELMETS AND FACEPLATES, IN RED OR YELLOW.

CAMERA SWEEPS ACROSS THE FIELD, FOCUSES ON PRUFROCK STANDING, ARMORED, HIS HELMET UNDER HIS ARM. HE LOOKS NERVOUS.

PRUFROCK: Well, here we are. The big day! I'm a bit nervous. But I feel good. Honestly, how can I turn down something like this? (smiles briefly) My insurance raised hell.

QUICK CUT TO THE SIDELINES, A MIDDLE AGED MAN IN A BLACK SUIT. SUBTITLE 'FILM'S INSURANCE AGENT.'

The Bear Cavalry — Page 142

****

CUT TO AN EARLIER SHOT - PRUFROCK IN A DRESSING ROOM, STANDING AGAINST THE WALL, DRESSED IN YELLOW PLASTIC ARMOUR. HE HAS A HELMET UNDER HIS ARM.

PRUFROCK: This is my playing outfit. It's like a suit of armor (laughs) if a suit of armor was bright red and made of plastic. It's actually very neat. Very comfortable.

HOLDS OUT THE HELMET.

PRUFROCK: Uhm... this helmet, it's rated stronger than a motorcycle helmet, or a football helmet. It's really made to take an impact. And these dangling straps, they are made to fix to the armor, so the helmet doesn't come off. Not without my whole head anyway (laughs).

PRUFROCK SHOWS OFF BOOTS, SHIN GUARDS, THIGH GUARDS, CROTCH PLATE, ARM GUARDS, SCALLOPED BREAST PLATE. HE TURNS AROUND TO SHOW THE SCALLOPED BACK PLATE.

PRUFROCK: This is really impressive. I could get hit by a car and walk away, wearing this.

PRUFROCK GIVES A THUMBS UP AND GRINS.

****

PRUFROCK: They actually suggested that I use a stunt double. (laughs) But really, this is a once in the lifetime thing.

ARN (coming into Camera frame and getting PRUFROCK in a headlock): its okay, Robin, we'll keep you safe. The other team, we will not let them near you.

PRUFROCK LAUGHS, PULLS OUT.

The Bear Cavalry – Page 143

ARN (looking at the camera): Robin will play backstop. Safest place on the field.

PRUFROCK: If you say so. (pause) Okay, I'm going to suit up. Did you want to explain the rules of the game.

CUT TO - COMPUTER GRAPHIC OF A PLAYING FIELD, AS ARN EXPLAINS THE TEAMS AND THE RULES FOR THE BALL.

CUT TO - Montage of scenes from previous games, as riders and bears chase the ball, sometimes pass the ball back and forth like basketball players, and occasional bruising collisions and swipes between animals.

CUT TO - Stridsvartabirni - The game is on! The riders and bears are rushing back and forth over the field, the ball rolling and batted this way and that. After ten minutes, the ball rolls into the backstop. For a moment, the ball is out in the open on its own.

Three riders converge, two red and one yellow. The voice over is a an Icelandic commentator, relating in a frenzy, there are no subtitles.

The yellow bear rears up and slaps one of the red riders in the chest with its paw, the rider goes flying.

AUDIENCE SHRIEKS. COMMENTATOR IS SCREAMING, ALMOST HYSTERICAL. THE ONLY LEGIBLE WORD IS 'PRUFROCK' REPEATED OVER ANDOVER.

The unhorsed Red bear rears up on its hind legs. The red and yellow bears exchange brutal slaps. Even the distance from the microphones, they pick up the 'swack, swack, swack' The Yellow Rider slides off his bear and backs away.

Some distance away, ROBIN PRUFROCK in his red armor lays on his back, and struggles to get up, but can't move.

The Red and Yellow bears abruptly go back on all fours and walk stiffly away from each other. The Yellow rider runs after to calm his bear. Game officials, and members of both teams are running to the spot. Among them are a trio of medical technicians in white, carrying a portable stretcher and an emergency kit.

PRUFROCK VOICE OVER: Just so you know. I wasn't killed.

CAMERA CLOSE UP OF THE ACCIDENT SCENE. PRUFROCK IS AT THE CENTRE OF THE MEDICS. THEY HOLD UP FINGERS, ASK QUESTIONS, HE ANSWERS. ONE OF THEM IS CUTTING THE ARMOUR OFF HIS BODY, SLICING THROUGH THE STRAPS.

ARN VOICE OVER: Is he dead? Check the helmet, is his head still in it?

JON VOICE OVER: No, no, his head is still on. Just the helmet came off.

ARN VOICE OVER: Good. Do you remember the quarter finals back five years ago.

JON VOICE OVER: Oh yeah. What was his name? Sven... something? Didn't his head come out of the helmet?

ARN VOICE OVER: No, it stayed in the helmet, but the helmet came off his body. Then the bears took it for the Olaf, and started batting it around. It took a while to get them to stop.

JON VOICE OVER: Look, he's alive.

ARN VOICE OVER: Oh good!

QUICK SHOT OF THE HELMET - THERE'S A CRACK RUNNING ACROSS ITS LENGTH.

QUICK SHOT OF AN UPPER BREASTPLATE, THE CENTRE IS SMASHED IN, CRACKS RUNNING THE LENGTH OF THE MOLDED PLASTIC.

PRUFROCK GLANCES AT THE CAMERA, AS THE MEDICS CHECK HIS NECK.

PRUFROCK: Did you get that? Did you get that? (whooshes breath) I didn't see it coming at all. One minute I'm riding, the next minute, it feels like I'm shot out of a cannon - Just POW!

MEDIC: Can you stand?

PRUFROCK: It felt like I was flying for ten minutes. I've never felt anything like that. What?

MEDIC: Can you stand?

PRUFROCK: I think so.

THE MEDICS HELP PRUFROCK STAND UP.

MEDIC: How does it feel? Do you feel anything? Do you want to take a step? Do you want us to hold you?

PRUFROCK TAKES A COUPLE OF STEPS. RAISES HIS ARMS. THE CROWD GOES WILD.

ARN: Robin, are you okay?

PRUFROCK: Good, (starting to breath heavily) I'm good. Maybe a little bruised. But I'm good. What a rush.

ARN: Robin, do you want to finish playing?

PRUFROCK: What? What? Yeah. Okay. I'm good.

FROM THE BACKGROUND, THE BLACK SUITED INSURANCE MAN COMES MARCHING FORWARD. HE'S VISIBLY AGITATED. HE WAVES AT THE CAMERA. HIS VOICE ISN'T LEGIBLE, BUT HE CAN BE SEEN ARGUING WITH GAME OFFICIALS AND TEAM MEMBERS, AT ONE POINT HE POINTS AT THE MEDICS. FINALLY, HE PICKS UP THE BROKEN BREASTPLATE AND HURLS IT TO THE GROUND, FOLDING HIS ARMS.

PRUFROCK VOICE OVER: And that was it, the Insurance Company wouldn't let me back in the game. In hindsight, I'm glad. I don't know what I was thinking.

CUT AWAY TO THE AFTER GAME. ALL THE TEAM MEMBERS, HALF OUT OF ARMOUR, ARE GATHERED AROUND PRUFROCK.

JON: Robin helped us win the game. The penalty to the yellow team allowed us to get ahead and we stayed ahead after that. Robin in appreciation, the team members wanted to give you this.

JON HANDS OVER A HEAVY GRAY LEATHER RAGGED SACK. ROBIN GRINS, ACCEPTING IT. HE TURNS IT AROUND, SO THAT THE CAMERA CAN SEE THE PAINTED FACE WITH THE HANDLEBAR MUSTACHE - IT IS THE BALL, OLAF, OR WHAT'S LEFT OF IT.

PRUFROCK: Gosh, thanks!

JON: Turn it around.

PRUFROCK TURNS THE TORN LEATHER OVER. THERE'S ILLEGIBLE MARKINGS ON IT.

ARN: All the team has signed it for you, ROBIN. To thank you for playing with us.

JON: And not being killed.

ARN (presenting a pen): It's your turn to sign now, ROBIN, to show you are part of our team!

TEAM CHEERS AS PRUFOCK SIGNS.

PRUFROCK VOICE OVER: The leather was a quarter of an inch thick, the bears were wearing muzzles and foot pads, and they still tore it open Luckily, we were able to sew Olaf up, and he came back to New York with me.

****

OPENING - CROWD SCENE, PEOPLE FILLING A STADIUM. THERE IS A PLATFORM.

PRUFROCK VOICE OVER: This is the Bear Show, the highlight of every Asbringnnastat - Bear Festival. This is what we've been waiting for.

THE CAMERA ZOOMS IN. HELGA, IN ARCHAIC DRESS COMES ONTO THE STAGE AND BOWS. THE CROWD CHEERS. SHE TURNS, AND EXTENDS HER ARM.

STIG THE BEAR, IMMENSE AND WEARING WOTAN'S ARMOUR, GLEAMING, BRONZED, JEWEL ENCRUSTED, COMES SHAMBLING OUT. STIG WALKS OVER TO STAND ON ALL FOURS BESIDE HELGA, LOOKING UP AT THE CROWD.

THE CHEERING GOES WILD. AMONG THE AUDIENCE, A CHANT SPRINGS UP.

WOTAN!

GATHERING FORCE, THE CALL TAKEN UP BY MANY THROATS.

WOTAN!!

WOTAN!!!

WOTAN!!!!

HELGA TAKES THREE STEPS AWAY, AND CLAPS HER HANDS TO ALERT STIG, HE LOOKS OVER IN HER DIRECTION. SHE RAISES UP HER ARM.

WOTAN!!!!

WOTAN!!!!!

WOTAN!!!!!!

THE BEAR RISES UP ON ITS HIND LEGS, STANDING OVER ELEVEN FEET TALL, DWARFING HELGA, DWARFING THE STAGE.

PRUFROCK VOICE OVER: This is magnificent!

THE CROWD GOES WILD, ROARING, CHANTING.

WOTAN!!!!!

WOTAN!!!!!

WOTAN!!!!!

The bear raises its forelegs, lifting them up high. It throws back its head and roars.

WOTAN!!!!!!!

FREEZE FRAME

THE END

ROLL CREDITS

The Bear Cavalry – Page 149

Afterword

I'm hoping that I don't have to say this, but I'll say it anyway. Just a reminder: This is a work of allo-historical fiction. In reality, bears were never domesticated, in Iceland or anywhere else. Bears have never been historically riding animals, a few circuses and some very drunk hooligans aside. Bear Cavalry has never ever existed, except as an internet meme. Don't ever try to ride a bear, they're not ponies.

This entire story has amounted to a historical 'what if' framed as a documentary movie. We hope that was entertaining.

As an allo-historical work, however, there is a great deal that is not fiction. Allow us to offer you a few footnotes here and there, for your entertainment, as to what was fact...

The Bear Necessities – Actual History

* Bears have been a totemic animal in Europe and especially Scandinavia going back to the dawn of history. Stone age relics suggest veneration of the bear.

* Early Norse Shaman's attempted to channel the spirit of bears. This lead directly to fighters wearing 'Bear Shirts', who became known as Berserkers. That's where Berserker comes from.

* There are a number of reports of brown bear cubs being adopted and raised as pets by Norse. In fact, the practice was not confined to the Norse. It appears elsewhere in Europe, particularly around the Baltics, in Germany and in Russia, wherever Bears were common. We even find it among North American Indians. The practice persisted into the 19th century in some areas, with mixed results. There are many, many stories of tame bears. The Norse seem particularly well known for it.

* The Norse Viking era and the Medieval Warm Period almost perfectly overlap. The theory that the Medieval Warm Period triggered the Viking era is recent and not entirely accepted, but I find it highly persuasive. Certainly the westward expansion and colonizations of Iceland and especially Greenland could have only happened during the Medieval Warm Period.

The Bear Cavalry – Page 151

* The chronicle of Norse expansion is essentially the history we know. In terms of exploration of North America, we know that they sailed as far as Baffin Island, which they called Helluland, the Labrador coast, which they called Markland, and Newfoundland, which they called Vinland. There is some suggestion they may have reached as far south as the Canadian Maritimes or the St. Laurence, but this is controversial.

* We do know that the Norse sailed from Greenland to Markland to harvest timber. Greenland lacked good forests. We don't know how many or how extensive these expeditions were, but they seem to have taken place over two centuries. But the Labrador coast was literally the only good source of timber for over a thousand miles.

* There is no indication or evidence that the Norse encountered black bears on the Labrador coast. But black bears are common in the region, and the Labrador black bear is the largest variety of black bear. There would have been a significant chance of encounters, although none are recorded.

* The distinctions and differences between the varieties of bears - particularly European brown bears, American black bears, polar bears, Grizzlies and Kodiaks are accurate by the way.

* Although the real world Norse never seem to have met or mentioned black bears, they went a bit wild for polar bears. There was an active trade in polar bear furs. Polar bear cubs from Greenland were taken and shipped to Europe as pets for Royalty and Popes, although the animals likely did not live long. We don't have records of the volume of polar bear furs or polar bear cubs, but it did happen at least on an occasional basis.

* The quotation from the early laws of Iceland concerning the keeping of tamed bears is accurate, feel free to look it up. In addition to eventually prohibiting brown bears, there are other laws referencing tame polar bears, and tame bears generally. The fact that Icelandic law makes a distinction between tame brown bears and tame bears generally suggests that a Black Bear or two might possibly have made it to Iceland, though there is no proof of this. What these laws really tell us is that the tradition of keeping tame bears seems to have been alive and well in Iceland, despite the bears having to be shipped all the way from either Greenland/Labrador on one side, or Norway/Sweden on the other. It also tells us that it happened often enough, or was common enough that the Icelanders felt they needed to make laws for it.

* The Bear Garden, also known as the Paris Garden, was a London entertainment establishment specializing in the torture or baiting of bears and other animals, bulls, dogs, apes, ponies, etc, that operated between 1560 and 1690. Bear baiting was a popular entertainment, the English monarchy had an appointed 'Bear Warden' since at least the 1400's.

* The English romantic poet, Lord George Gordon Byron, while attending Trinity College from 1805 to 1808, kept a tame bear with him. Apparently, this was because dogs weren't allowed at Trinity College. According to reports, Byron would take the bear out for walks with him, with the animal on a leash like a dog. He was apparently quite fond of it, and took it with him when he left Trinity. Byron over his life accumulated quite a menagerie of animals.

* The Norse decline is closely associated with the end of the Medieval Warm period and the ensuing cold periods, and certainly there's records of climate related decline in Norway,

Greenland and Iceland. But it's also likely that the continuing evolution and adaptation, technological innovation and increasing state complexity in Europe was going to spell the end for the Norse.

* The meat of black bears was prized by Native Americans prior to and after European contact. It was also a favorite of European colonists. During the New Amsterdam period, bear meat was so popular or plentiful that the 'Bear Market' was established for it - this is the origin of the Wall street term.

* Teddy Roosevelt did in fact kill and eat both Black Bear meat and Grizzly meat, and wrote about both. Teddy did considered black bear far superior to grizzly, which he described as rough and tasteless. Black bear he compared to pork.

* The role and status of pigs in Scandinavian society is as described. Pig raising seems to have been somewhat climate sensitive, and so was most widespread in the southern reaches of Scandinavia, particularly Denmark and lower Norway and Sweden. Pigs were known to have been raised, however, in both Iceland and Greenland during the warm period. In both cases, pigs disappeared as the climate worsened.

FINISHED

Monarchs Behaving Badly – Actual History

* The description of the evolution of the Danish, Swedish, and Norwegian kingdoms, and the various Monarchs and successions leading up to the Kalmar Union and Margaret and Erik is essentially taken from real life. As noted, the detailed history is baroque, but this cliff notes version is sufficient for our purposes.

* The Kalmar Union, 1397 to 1523, was a 'joint kingdom or confederacy' of Denmark, Sweden and Norway, including Finland, the Faeroe Islands, Iceland and Greenland. The three kingdoms were technically separate, but all ruled by the same king. Unlike Great Britain, the internal divisions were never resolved and it eventually broke apart, with Sweden pursuing an Empire around the Baltic Sea and Denmark ruling Norway, Iceland and the north Atlantic.

* Margaret 1 of Denmark, born 1353, and acknowledged as the 'first great ruling Queen of European history.' The youngest daughter of King Valdemar of Denmark, at the age of ten, she became 'Queen Consort' of Norway in 1363, and then of Sweden, in 1364. Following her father's death she had her five year old son, Olaf, elected King of Denmark in 1375, and ruled through him. She later elevated Olaf to King of Norway in 1380, continuing to rule through him. Olaf died in 1387, but that didn't slow her down. In 1389, after a war, she

became ruler of Sweden. She appointed her nephew, Eric of Pomerania, to the thrones of the three Kingdoms, but continued to rule directly until her death in 1412.

* Eric of Pomerania, 1381-1459. The description and the background of the Boy King, Eric, appears accurate from what we know of him. Descriptions of Eric as an adult emphasize his charm, intelligence and 'vision' or creative imagination. They also emphasize his impulsiveness, recklessness, short temper and easy frustration and stubbornness. These qualities have been extrapolated back to the likely character of a teenage youth. Although Margaret was intent on retaining her grip on power until her death, she seems to have been serious on ensuring the survival of the Union, and on making sure that Eric was properly educated and trained

* Henry III and Henry IV, the Counts of Stauffenberg and Holstein, along with their brothers, are genuine historical characters, and the descriptions of the wars between them and the Kalmar Union, and Margaret and Eric is accurate though superficial, up to 1426. When you start getting into the various claims and statuses of European nobility and royalty, their kinships and relationships, and their claims on different pieces of territory it turns into a snake pit of reductionism. The geopolitics were essentially accurate - sea landings were no easier then than now. If you wanted to move an army, it had to be overland, and the provinces of the Danish Peninsula were a major obstacle to the Kalmar Union's expansion.

* The stresses between Denmark and Sweden over the German wars are accurate. The role of Queen Philippa in holding the Union together, and particularly holding Sweden in the Union is also accurate. With the loss of Philippa, Eric

lost a lot of his diplomatic edge - more damage was done with his choice of Philippa's handmaiden as his consort, there were rumors that she had murdered Philippa. The farmers and miners revolts in Sweden, and the peasants revolt in Norway are accurate, although Bear Cavalry was obviously not deployed.

* In real life, Eric did not succeed in getting his cousin Boguslaw appointed as his heir. Eric was actually succeeded by Christopher of Bavaria. Christopher took a while getting elected by the various councils of nobles - Denmark, 1440, Norway, 1441 and Sweden 1442. It was Christopher who fought the peasant rebellion in Jutland. He died as in 1448, being replaced by Christian.

* As for Eric himself, his fate in real life is a little different. Eric was unable to get Boguslaw appointed as his replacement. In frustration, he basically quit as King, in 1439, retreating to a fortress on the Island of Gottland in the Baltic Sea, where he spent the next ten years as a kind of pirate lord, terrorizing and looting shipping, and generally pissing people off. He was deposed by Sweden and Denmark in 1439 and Norway in 1440, not that it mattered to him, because he'd already quit. Eventually, in 1449, Christian persuaded him to stop being a prick, give up piracy, leave Gottland and return to Pomerania, replacing Boguslaw as Duke. He lived for another ten years. I'm not making this up.

* The war between Denmark and Sweden, and between Charles II and Christian I, ended about the same way in real life, though less one sided. Christian I's rule in Sweden did not last nearly as long. Charles II was not beheaded by a bear, and instead lived to be King of Sweden twice more. Swedish centrifugalism was already well established. Christian II's reign in real life was one of violent blunder. Frederick's rule

was about dealing with Christian II's legacy, and most of Christian III's was about fighting revolts initially, until he just got sick of war.

* Following the end of the Kalmar Union, Sweden became a regional superpower, building an empire around the Baltic and fighting a series of wars in with German states, with Poland, Lithuania, and Russia, between 1550 and 1750, collectively called the Northern Wars. Sweden had the advantage of very good leadership, military tactics that were well ahead of its time, and consistently punched above its weight class, but it eventually lost out to Russia. Honestly, the entire medieval period of European history, from 1300 to 1800 is just mental, there are so many wars, between so many states, that it's amazing that they were able to keep it all straight. I'm sure there was probably some occasion when some European monarch showed with his army to an empty field because he accidentally declared war on himself.

* Denmark became heavily involved in European affairs, most notably the thirty years war. It eventually opted to become a sea empire. In addition to Norway, Iceland and Greenland, it established colonies and trading posts in Africa, in India, in the West Indies, and in the Baltic. It couldn't compete with Britain, and most of its possessions were scooped up by the English in the 19th century. The Danish Virgin Islands in the Caribbean were acquired by the United States in 1917.

* After the Kalmar Union broke up in 1521, Norway tried for independence but was conquered by Denmark, and it remained a Danish possession until 1814, and the Napoleonic wars. From 1814 to 1905, it was forced into a loose union with Sweden.

* Iceland was originally independent, until it affiliated with Norway. When Norway was joined with Denmark, Iceland was along for the ride. Norwegian independence did not affect Iceland, which remained under the control of Denmark until 1944. Greenland continues to remain associated with Iceland.

* Although there was never such a thing as Bear Cavalry, the discussions of early firearms, firearm tactics and military tactics, though superficial, is correct.

* Finally - Robin Prufrock's caution is correct and should always be followed. Bears are dangerous wild animals, always treat them with respect, do not approach or harass them, avoid contact if you can.

And never, ever try and ride one.

FINISHED

BONUS STORY

The Sharebear Apocalypse

OPENING - A news desk with two local news casters, Tom Nabors and Merica Johnson, a regional news hour.

ZOOM IN on the male Newscaster in the center, middle aged, blandly handsome, carefully coiffed. Tom Nabors:

NABORS: ....And that's the news for Chicago. Turning now to the human interest side of life, we have Merica Johnson, who went into the field with this evening's in-depth feature about Chicago's newest invasive species, and for once, it's a welcome one. Chicago, say hello to the ... Sharebears.

CUT TO MERICA JOHNSON, blonde, perky, on a busy Chicago street. Beside her, holding her free hand, is a grinning Sharebear, and with it, a pair of smiling children and their mother.

MERICA: Thank you... Jim. Yes, Chicago has a new invasive species, and for once, Chicagoans couldn't be happier. The windy city is for once, opening its arms wide for a hug for the Sharebears...

CUT TO montage of file footage clips, rats, pigeons, rabbits, raccoons, skunks. A shot of a coyote slinking down a street. Deer munching in peoples lawns.

MERICA (VOICE OVER): The urban environment is home not just to people and their pets, but to a variety of ride along animals. Animals which have adapted to city life and people. We have rats and pigeons of course, but in the last few decades, skunks, raccoons and even deer have adapted to the urban and suburban way of life. Mostly, they just stay out of our way, or are considered pests and troublemakers. But not these little fellows.

MONTAGE SHIFT - shots of Sharebears and children playing in a park. A garbage man pausing on his rounds to hand out sandwiches to Sharebears. A busy executive pausing on his rounds to exchange a hug.

CUT TO INTERVIEW WITH GARBAGE MAN, standing next to his garbage truck

MERICA: Do they ever cause trouble? Are they ever a nuisance?

GARBAGE MAN: Well they tip over some trash now and then, you can understand they might get hungry. But no. They're not like rats or raccoons. It's nice having them around. We don't mind picking up after them now and then, it's just a little thing.

MERICA: What happened to your hand?

GARBAGE MAN: Oh this? (Holds up a bandaged hand, missing fingers) Caught it in the machinery. It's a risky job sometimes. No big deal, doesn't hurt at all.

MERICA: The Sharebears aren't a distraction.

GARBAGE MAN (laughs): Not at all. It's nice having them around. It brightens up my day. My wife has taken to packing extra sandwiches for the little rascals.

CLOSE UP ON MERICA, addressing the camera.

MERICA: So what exactly are Sharebears? Where do they come from? Why are they so gosh darned friendly and loveable? To find out, we went to the experts...

CUT TO MERICA in what looks like a laboratory office. Caption identifies a man in a white lab coat as "Doctor Penfield Stangwild - Expert on Sharebears." Doctor Stangwild wears an eye patch and has heavy scarring down one side of his face, testament to a previous history of working with dangerous animals.

MERICA: Doctor Stangwild, are Sharebears actually bears?

STANGWILD: (laughs) Oh no, not at all. They're not related to the genus Ursus. What they are is an offshoot of Mustelids, a Procyonidae - their closest relatives are raccoons and badgers, and of course, skunks (chuckles). The resemblance to bears is remarkable, but that's a result of parallel evolution - having much the same lifestyle and diet - on average, Sharebears are a tenth or less the size of real bears. And of course (chuckles) real bears are much more dangerous.

MERICA: You said similar lifestyle?

STANGWILD: Yes. Well, Sharebears are order carnivore, like dogs, felines and bears of course, but despite that, they're basically omnivores. Like bears, a large part of their diet comes from vegetation. Like Bears, they're basically forest dwellers, going through seasonal phases. I believe that they originated in the Pacific Northwest.

MERICA (interrupting): I guess the question everyone wants to know is why they're so darned cute!

STANGWILD: Oh... Oh... Sorry. A lot of reasons, I think. They're plantigrades, partially bipedal, like Bears they can stand up on their hind legs and walk. They actually walk better and further than bears. Even more than apes at times. So there's a humanlike quality there that attracts people. Of course they're small, so harmless - an average Sharebear is around sixty pounds. And then there's the appearance - the whole 'Disney' thing - they have large eyes, short muzzles, rounded features. Their vocalisations sound a lot like happy children laughing or playing. And of course, there's the 'Sharebear Share' which is hard to resist (chuckles).

CLOSE UP ON MERICA - ADDRESSING CAMERA

MERICA: Whatever the reason, the Sharebears make friends no matter where they go.

INTERVIEW: KENNELS, mostly empty. Subtitle, 'Animal control.' A second subhead identifies the person Merica is talking to - Vic Wakin, Manager.

MERICA: So you're the head of the Chicago's animal control department?

WAKIN: That's right Ma'am, twenty years now.

MERICA: So you must have seen a lot of animal cases, not just stray dogs and cats.

WAKIN: Mostly dogs and cats, but just about everything. Lots of raccoons and skunks. Skunks are bad. Some coyotes. Deer even. There was a python once, someone abandoned in a hotel room. And then there was even one time a cougar wandered into the city. Vermin, hate em all.

MERICA: What about Sharebears?

WAKIN (visibly lightening up and breaking into a grin): Well, now that's a different thing. I remember the first time we saw one - had a call for a bear in a back yard. Figured it was a real bear. Those things are dangerous, you get a bear, it's a crisis. We were loaded up, tranquillizers, shotguns, a big bear trap...

The Bear Cavalry — Page 165

we get there, and it's just a little thing. At first I thought it was a cub or something. But then, damned if it didn't get up on its hind legs, walk over and give me a hug. Everyone laughed! (Wakins smiles at the memory)

MERICA: Are Sharebears a problem?

WAKIN: No problem at all. They're as harmless as can be. Unless you don't like hugs.

MERICA: But don't they cause a nuisance? Dig up things, get into trash, make nests, poop?

WAKIN: Oh not so you'd notice, it's never anything to get all worked up over.

MERICA: So no one minds?

WAKIN: Well, I suppose some do, but you know, they're just Grumps. Grumps we like to call em down here. And the thing is, Sharebears, they do a lot of good.

MERICA: How so?

WAKIN: Well, they're just so darn adorable you know. But besides that, I can tell you that since the Sharebears started showing up, we hardly get any calls for raccoons or skunks, it's like they just take off. Hell, we pick up hardly any stray dogs even.

TRACKING SHOT OF LONG ROW OF EMPTY DOG POUND KENNELS

WAKIN: All I can say is that I'm all right with the Sharebears. I wish there were twice as many.

MERICA: Twice as many?

WAKIN: They just make you feel good, you know. You feel good having them around.

SCENES OF MOUNTAINS AND GREEN PACIFIC RAIN FORESTS

MERICA (VOICE OVER): Originally, Sharebears were native to the American northwest. Their range was the hills and valleys of the Rockies, from British Colombia to as far south as Oregon, where they were beloved by the Native People.

CUT TO: A Native American elder sitting in front of a Haida village, totem poles and long houses, the Rockies rising majestically behind him. Close up on the Elder.

ELDER: The animals you call Sarh-bears, we knew them as Wish-Santa-Eh-Way. They were a very spiritual animal. Very powerful magic. We were taught, you must always be respectful of the Wish-Santa-Way. You could only approach them from behind. And if they saw you, you must run away as fast as you can. The lands of the Wish-Santa-Way were forbidden to men, we did not go into them.

CUT TO SHOT: MERICA in a laboratory setting. On the wall behind her are a series of larger than life diagrams of Sharebears and Sharebear anatomy. With her is a tall man in a white lab coat, balding. Zoom in.

MERICA: This is Doctor Stanton, an expert in biochemistry. Doctor Stanton, I understand that you're also an expert on Sharebears.

STANTON: In a manner of speaking.

MERICA: Doctor Stanton, we've heard a lot about the 'Sharebear Share' what can you tell us about that?

STANTON: Well, technically speaking, it's not a share at all. It's a chemical defense mechanism. Like a skunk.

MERICA: A skunk! Oh no

The Bear Cavalry – Page 167

STANTON: It's a defense mechanism, Merica. Like skunks, Sharebears don't have much in the way of teeth or claws; they're not very fast comparatively, so they need a way to defend themselves from attackers. Sharebears are related to skunks, and they've evolved a very similar defense mechanism. Skunks discharge a powerful noxious chemical from their anal glands.

MERICA (looking off camera): Can we say anal on the news?

STANTON (ignoring her): As I said, SKUNKS discharge from ANAL glands. A lot of animals have ANAL glands. But Sharebears, instead of discharging from ANAL glands, discharge from a pair of modified NIPPLES on their upper torso. Skunks lift their tails, Sharebears rear up on their hind legs and spread their forelimbs wide (demonstrates).

MERICA: Now nipples. We may have to edit this.

STANTON (irritably): Yes, Merica. NIPPLES. The big difference between Sharebears and Skunks though, it's not just about NIPPLES and ANAL glands, is in the chemical nature of the discharge.

MERICA: And what is that? We all know skunks are pretty noxious.

STANTON: Correct, skunks are... as you say 'noxious.' The Sharebears chemical discharge, however, is a psychoactive.

MERICA: You mean like a perhomone.

STANTON: (sighs): No, not a pheromone. A psychoactive chemical, loosely related to opiates. The molecule is coupled to a neurotoxin, so it works either inhaled or through skin contact. It brings about a feeling of tranquility, wellbeing, passivity, aggression vanishes, and while it's not a full paralytic motor coordination declines.

The Bear Cavalry – Page 168

MERICA: So skunks spray a terrible odor, and Sharebears spray a feel-good. Isn't that amazing? Sharebears defend themselves from attack by making their enemies feel good.

STANTON: It's not unlimited, each Sharebear has maybe a dozen or so shots, and then their bodies have to manufacture more. That's why Sharebears will often line up beside each other, together, to discharge. The more animals, the more intense the discharge. The less strain on each individual. And the fewer chances of a miss.

STANTON: Well, there's more to it than that. It's incredibly potent stuff, even a trace amount strongly affects behavior. As I've said, it's linked to a neurotoxin for skin absorption, and it's surrounded with an oil base, so if it gets on you it clings, which extends the effect.

MERICA: Oh.

STANTON: That's why Sharebears like to hug. It's in the area of the oddly shaped patch of fur.

MERICA: The heart shape?

STANTON: In some, yes, it resembles a heart shape. Sometimes a triangle, or a starfish, or a cloud, it's actually just random. It's a specialized patch of hair follicles that hold the discharge, and are used to rub it into the subject.

MERICA: That's just amazing. Doctor Stanton, I want to thank you for your time. There you have it folks. Aren't the Sharebears just the most wonderful little things ever!

BACK TO NEWS DESK - MERICA AND NABORS

CLOSE UP ON NABORS, HE TURNS TO CAMERA

NABORS: The Pacific Northwest is a long way away from the Windy City. How did they get here? The answer is in the Sharers.

CUT TO: Exterior - windy day, overcast, the wind is making popping noises on the microphone. A Winnebago pulls up to a playground, riding over the parking dividers with a lurch before coming to a stop. A group of children cease playing, their mothers stepping forward protectively.

The Winnebago door opens, and a group of Sharebears file out. They mill around. Seeing the children, they open their arms wide for a hug. After hesitation, the children run to embrace the sharebears. Mothers beam happily.

VOICE OVER, CLOSE UP ON AN UNKEMPT BEARDED MIDDLE AGED MAN, SOMEWHAT EMACIATED, TALKING TO NABORS

NABORS (VO): This is Dave Mundy. Dave is part of a network of 'Sharers men and women who have made it their life's work to bring the Sharebears to the world.

MUNDY: That's right, Tom. Me and the family, we've been bringing the good news, introducing these adorable creatures to the wide world.

NABORS: How long have you and your family been doing this?

MUNDY: Oh, I'd say going on twelve, fifteen years now. You lose track. I think we might be the first Sharers, me and Doris and the kids. (Looks vaguely off camera) I used to have a job, right. And a house. But you just get called right? You fill with purpose, and you go where the lord wants you to go. And the lord wants us to spread these little fellows around. There's not enough love in the world, and god sent them to redress that balance. And god sent us to help them get their message out there.

NABORS: How did you happen to do it?

MUNDY: Well we were on vacation, me and the family, in the Northwest, and we just came across these little fellas. We were pulled up, and having dinner? Out in the wild, you know? And I think... I think... I think... My daughter, Angie, she came back to camp, and she had one of the little guys with her. She said 'He's my new friend, he's hungry, can he have supper with us.' He looked like a bear cub, I was concerned there was a mother bear around. I shooed everyone in the trailer. I said, 'Angie, come away from that.' But she wouldn't, she just said over and over, 'He's my new friend.' Then the little fellow got right up on his hind legs, and walked right up to me and gave me a big hug. Suddenly, I knew it was all right. So I called the family out, and it was amazing, he gave each of us a hug, just like a person. I could tell he didn't mean no harm, so we treated him just like a human guest. And others came along, and soon we were feeding a pile of them. They just kept coming. And we kept staying, making new friends. Until the food ran out.

MUNDY'S SMILE IS BEATIFIC

MUNDY: So then Delores, that's... that was my wife, she said we had to go get food. But we didn't want to be away from them. So she said 'let's take them with us!' And off we went. Everyone loved them, everyone we met, they loved them just like we did. A few got tired of travelling with us, they made so many new friends, I guess, they just wanted to stay. And we kept travelling... That's how it started.

NABORS: So you're not working?

MUNDY: No, not since we started sharing.

The Bear Cavalry – Page 171

NABORS: How do you support yourself and your family now?

MUNDY (SMILING): When you share love, people give you what you need. I go into a gas station, a grocery store, and all of a sudden, there's so much love and goodwill, people give me money, food, I fill up the gas at the pump, and the clerk won't even take money for it. That's the effect these little guys have. It's as if Jesus himself was walking with us.

CUT TO: CCTV camera showing a gas bar lot, featuring rows of pumps, as the Winnebago pulls up. The Winnebago door flies open. A man staggers out, followed by a small horde of sharebears scampering about. Cars pull away, or swerve to avoid entering the lot. A pair of sharebears run up to a man pumping gas in his car, pulling him down. The gas nozzle falls to the pavement, still pumping away, as the man frolics with the two sharebears. His shirt begins to stain red, but he is not bothered. Some of the bears on all fours race into the gas bar's convenience store.

CUT TO: CCTV interior of the convenience store, the bears are scampering up and down the aisles pulling products from the shelves and scattering them about, tearing open packages. One of them manages to open the cooler section. Bottles and cartons are flung about, until it finds its way to the ice cream. The humans in the store watch without any signs of terror or distress, as the animals run riot.

NABORS: Can they be destructive?

MUNDY: They're high spirited, I'll admit that, but they don't mean no harm.

NABORS: What about your family? Where are they? Do they still ride along with you?

MUNDY'S SMILE FLICKERS - for the first time, he looks uncertain. He tries to focus, his brow furrowing. And then it fades.

MUNDY: They're not around any more...

SLOWLY, MUNDY'S PLACID EXPRESSION RETURNS, HE STOPS THINKING ABOUT THEM.

CUT BACK TO NEWS DESK - MERICA BEAMS AT TOM.

MERICA: Well, from the gas station footage, it seems like they sure can be a handful, those frisky camps.

NABORS: Yes indeed, but you can tell from the footage, and I can verify from talking to people, that no one seems to mind.

MERICA: What's a little mess, after all, right?

NABORS: Exactly, what's a little mess?

MERICA: It can always be cleaned up. No big deal. And it's a small price to pay for these adorable visitors.

NABORS: That's right Merica.

MERICA: Chicago's got quite a population of these friendly critters now, would you say?

NABORS: Well, we couldn't get a hard answer from anyone, but the consensus seems to be that there aren't enough of them yet. They haven't worn out their welcome in Chicago. And I don't think they will for some time to come.

MERICA: Chicago's welcomed them with open arms. Even into people's homes.

CUT TO: ESTABLISHING SHOT IN A ROW OF TOWNHOUSES.

CUT TO: INTERIOR IN A RESIDENTIAL LIVING ROOM, ESTABLISHING SHOT, MERICA SITTING IN AN OVERSTUFFED CHAIR, WITH A MIDDLE AGED MARRIED COUPLE, LEANING FORWARD OVER COFFEE.

MERICA: I just want to say, this is good coffee!

MAN: Thank you, Merica. (Caption identifies him as Sydney Blasco)

A GOLD FURRED SHAREBEAR WALKS UP TO MERICA ON ALL FOURS, YEARS AND GIVES HER A HUG. MERICA MAKES A SURPRISED NOISE. THE SHAREBEAR'S CLAWS DRAG ALONG HER SHOULDER, TEARING HER JACKET AND BLOUSE. FOR A MOMENT, A BREAST IS EXPOSED, NIPPLE PROMINENT, BUT ALWAYS PROFESSIONAL, SHE COVERS IT. THE CLAWS LEAVE RED WOUNDS DOWN HER SHOULDER, BUT SHE DOESN'T SEEM TO NOTICE.

MERICA: (Laughs) That was surprising! I guess this is the newest member of the family?

WOMAN: We call him Jake. (Caption identifies her as Marion Blasco) Actually, our son Anton named him. Brought him home one day. Just like that. He was so friendly, he was like family. He was practically a person. We brought him a chair, he sat right at the dinner table with us. He slept in Anton's room that night, it was as if they'd been best friends their whole lives.

SYDNEY: We weren't sure what to do. I mean, it is a wild animal, right?

MARION SLAPS HIS KNEE REPROACHFULLY

SYDNEY: But winter is coming, and it's getting pretty cold out there. We were worried that the little guy might have a tough time of it.

MARION: Anton insisted that he stay with us, just for the winter. So he'd be safe.

SYDNEY: Well, that's a little unusual, sheltering a wild anim– anim– .... But hey, we had plenty of room, right.

CAMERA PANS ACROSS THE ROOM - THERE ARE VISIBLE CLAW MARKS ON THE WALLS, THE FURNITURE IS TORN, WITH STUFFING RIPPED OUT, THERE ARE FAECES ON THE FLOOR ALONG THE WALLS. WHEN SYDNEY SCRATCHES HIS LEG, HIS PANTS LEG LIFTS, SHOWING A HEAVY BANDAGE JUST ABOVE THE ANKLE.

THE SHAREBEAR MOVES TOWARDS THE CAMERA, WHICH SHAKES SUDDENLY. THE WORDS 'GET AWAY FROM ME!' CAN BE HEARD FROM THE NEWS CAMERA. THE SHAREBEAR VEERS AWAY.

MARION, SYDNEY AND MERICA LOOK TOWARDS THE CAMERA. SHE LOOKS CONCERNED.

MERICA: Are you okay, Billy? You didn't kick it, did you?

BILLY (VO): No, no. It just surprised me, that's all.

MARION: (laughs) That's Jake. I swear, he's the friendliest thing you ever saw.

BILLY (VO): (interrupting) Merica, are you okay.

MERICA'S SCRATCHES ARE BLEEDING, SHE HASN'T NOTICED. HER HAND IS STILL COVERING HER EXPOSED BREAST. SHE LOOKS IRRITATED AT

THE INTERRUPTION. SHE RETURNS TO THE
INTERVIEW.

MERICA: I'm fine Billy. Now, Marion...

BILLY (VO): (interrupting) Merica, I think you're bleeding.

MERICA LOOKS IRRITATED AGAIN.

MARION: (seeming to notice) Oh dear! How did that
happen! Let me get something to put on that for you.

MARION GETS UP AND LEAVES FOR THE
KITCHEN. CAMERA WATCHES HER GO. SHE LIMPS
A LITTLE. JAKE FOLLOWS HER INTO THE
KITCHEN.

MERICA: Now where were we? Yes, I can certainly see that
Jake is friendly.

SYDNEY: (Continuing) Loves people. Loves animals. He's
just best friends with our little dog Perkins.

BILLY (VO): (interrupting) I haven't seen a dog around here.

SYDNEY: Oh he's around here somewhere. He just loves
Jake. We all love Jake. Why, he could be my own son... if my
son was hairy and went around on all fours sometime.

BILLY (VO): Anton, that's your son right. Where is he right
now?

SYDNEY: At school, I guess. That boy studies hard.

BILLY (VO): It's Saturday.

SYDNEY LOOKS BLANK.

BILLY (VO): It's Saturday, there's no school on Saturday.
Sydney.... listen carefully to me. Where's Anton?

SYDNEY SEEMS TO THINK, CONCENTRATING.

SYDNEY: I guess... I guess... He must be... (brightens) He's up in his room!

MARION: (Returning, with a white towel and some medical tape on a tray.) What?

JAKE FOLLOWS HER FROM THE KITCHEN.

SYDNEY: Anton, he's up in his room.

MARION: (Smiling, as if having been reminded) Oh... that's where he is. Such a good boy. He brought Jake into our family. Did you know that? Walked right through that door with him.

BILLY (VO): If I went to Anton's room... what would I find?

MARION AND SYDNEY LOOK BLANK. MERICA IS PRESSING THE WHITE CLOTH TO HER SHOULDER, SHE'S LOOKING INCREASINGLY UNCOMFORTABLE.

SYDNEY: (Hesitating) Anton's up in his room.

BILLY (VO): I'm going up to Anton's room.

MERICA: Billy! Enough!

PATTING MARION'S KNEE, LEANING FORWARD TO THE TWO OF THEM.

MERICA: I'm so sorry. I promise, we'll edit this part out.

CUT BACK TO STUDIO, MERICA AND NABORS AT THEIR NEWS DESK.

NABORS: Well, it seems that Chicagoans are opening their homes as well as their hearts. It's a beautiful thing.

MERICA: That's right, Tom. The Sharebears are here to stay. There may be some downside, but I can tell you, their greatest gift is to bring out the best in people!

NABORS: And that's our show.

MERICA: (laughs) Not quite Tom, to bring things to a close, we have a surprise special guest to say hello.

NABORS: (laughing) Oh that's right. Bring him out!

FROM OFF CAMERA, ACCOMPANIED BY A HANDLER WHO IS NOMINALLY HOLDING A LEASH, A SHAREBEAR, LIGHT BROWN IN COLOUR, COMES WADDLING OUT IN A FOUR LEGGED GAIT. IT SEEMS CONFUSED BY THE LIGHTS, REARING UP ON TWO LEGS AND DROPPING BACK TO FOUR FEET, AGAIN AND AGAIN. FINALLY, IT TURNS TOWARDS THE CAMERA, REARS UP, AND SPREADS IT'S ARMS WIDE FOR A HUG.

****

THREE YEARS LATER

YOUTUBE - VIDEO - TITLE: SHAREBEARS MEET BAMBI

EIGHT MINUTES LONG POSTED BY NATUREFACT

VIDEO shows a young white tailed deer in the forest.

NARRATOR: Okay, now watch this.

VIDEO: The deer looks up, the ears flicker, the tail elevates, we can see tension in the body, as it prepares to flee.

NARRATOR: It senses danger.

VIDEO: The deer takes off bounding a few steps and then stops, trembling and uncertain. A sharebear is ahead of it. The deer stares at the bear uncertainly. The sharebear is upright on two legs, with its arms spread wide. The deer looks around, apparently distressed but unwilling to move. From behind, another sharebear moves towards the deer, also upright, with its arms spread.

NARRATOR: Now this is interesting. Did you see that? The bears were working together. Classic hunting behaviour, like a wolf pack. One bear startles the deer and sends it fleeing into the ambush.

VIDEO: The deer retreats slowly as the sharebears advance, a third and then a fourth one comes into frame, each walking upright. They approach the deer, which seems uncertain, but does not try and flee. First one sharebear, and then the others embrace the deer. Eventually, the deer starts licking and nuzzling the bears as they crowd around it.

NARRATOR This is amazing.

VIDEO: One of the sharebears is biting and clawing at the deer's flank. Blood is clearly flowing. The deer shows no sign of distress, continuing to lick one of the sharebears affectionately. The other bears follow suit, a slow motion feeding frenzy. The deer wobbles and then goes down, again showing no sign of distress.

NARRATOR: Dear god.

VIDEO: One of the sharebears appears to be digging into its stomach. Loops of intestine are briefly seen. There is blood everywhere. The deer blinks, and tries to nuzzle the bears affectionately. It displays no awareness that it is slowly being torn to pieces.

NARRATOR: I can't believe what I'm seeing. These things are all over the place now. I saw one the other day in a park where kids were playing.

VIDEO: Sharebears feeding...

 end.

****

FIVE YEARS LATER

SHARECROWS NEST - A MESSAGE BOARD,

ELIAN: It's not just a North American problem. They're in Brazil.

ROBIN: What? How the hell did they get down there? Ship?

ELIAN: No, flew down. Apparently, one of these Sharers bought three of them tickets as children. They walked right through the terminal, right through security, no one did anything. On the plane, they freaked out and ate a stewardess and nobody was the least bit bothered.

MIKE: Goddammed Sharer!

SANDIP: That shit goes way beyond pheromones, or neurotoxins or whatever. I swear those things have some kind of psychic power.

NIGEL: Nope, all chemistry. They're just animals. They're not even any smarter than raccoons or apes or creatures like that.

ELIAN: Yeah, so there's a colony of them in Brazil, ended up in the Barrios, where the poor people just love them. Government tried to eradicate them, riots went on for three days.

NIGEL: I've heard of colonies in Europe. They're in London, France, Berlin. Apparently, in Berlin, they were in a zoo, that didn't turn out so good. Even Moscow. I heard that they were doing biological research.

ELIAN: These things are just getting everywhere. I tell you, we need to be worried.

SANDIP: I don't think they'll show up in places like Calcutta or Lagos, they'd just eat them there. Riyadh's too hot for them.

NIGEL: You ever look at the growth projections. Active predator, high reproduction rate, no enemies. Hell, we end up protecting them. There's no limit.

MOD: I've warned you about fearmongering.

****

SIX YEARS LATER

YOUTUBE - VIDEO - TITLE: SHARING WITH SHAREBEARS

NINE MINUTES LONG POSTED BY BRONWIN

VIDEO: shows a mother pushing a baby carriage out for a stroll in the park. A sharebear walks up to her. She stops to pet it, kneeling down.

MOTHER: Hello fella, how are you?

VIDEO: It licks her face and she laughs. As she tries to stand, it wraps its arms around her in a hug. She pauses a second and then disengages herself, standing upright. The Sharebear rubs itself against her leg like a cat, and pushes at her hand with its muzzle.

The Bear Cavalry – Page 181

MOTHER: You sure are friendly. Do you want a treat? I'm sorry, I don't have anything. I'm sorry.

VIDEO: The sharebear licks her hand. Nuzzling it. The baby cries. Another sharebear approaches.

MOTHER: I'm sorry, I don't have anything to feed you...

VIDEO: She pets the second sharebear, as it sniffs around, its nose poking at her knees, at the other bear, at the carriage. The two sharebears touch noses.

MOTHER: You guys are so hungry! That's awful! I wish I had something... Wait, I know.

VIDEO: The mother pulls a baby bottle from the carriage.

MOTHER: Here, I have something. Here you go!

VIDEO: She squirts milk at the first bear, wetting its muzzle. It licks its muzzle and opens its mouth wide. She squirts milk into its mouth, and then into the open mouth of the second bear.

MOTHER: Here you go, here you go, here for each of you, you babies like that. Yes you do. You like that.

VIDEO: Two more Sharebears are approaching. The mother doesn't pay attention, instead focusing on squirting milk into their open mouths, and cooing and laughing.

MOTHER: That's it babies, drink up. That's it. You like that. I know you do! This is the good stuff. It's not formula. It's straight from mommy herself. I pumped this morning. Oh yes yes yes, you love it! I know you do.

VIDEO: The other two sharebears have arrived, she squirts milk into their mouths, alternating among the four of them, and laughing. One of them grabs at her hand with its forepaws, wrestling the baby bottle away from her. It takes

The Bear Cavalry – Page 182

several comical steps away, holding the bottle in its forepaws, and then rolls onto its back to suckle from the bottle.

VIDEO: The baby is crying. The camera returns to the carriage. One of the sharebears is hugging the mother, who is returning the hug, bending forward, wrapping her arms around the creature. Another rears up, and she hugs it. The third Sharebear is becoming interested in the carriage, poking its nose. The baby cries louder.

MOTHER: What's that? What's that?

VIDEO: The hugs are over. Now two sharebears are rearing up to poke their noses into the carriage. The third is examining the wheels of the carriage.

MOTHER: Oh you guys! You've never seen a baby! Want to see? Want to see?

VIDEO: She takes the baby out of the carriage and bends down, holding it out for the Sharebears to see. They all rear up on their hind legs. Two of them reach out with forepaws. One of them pulls the baby from her, holding it in its forelimbs.

MOTHER: Oopsy! You want to hold him. You hold him. That's a good boy. Look at you. You're holding him just like mommy.

VIDEO: The sharebear turns to walk away, not hurried this time, but clumsily walking upright carrying the baby. The other three sharebears, including the one that was sucking on the bottle, follow after, together with the mother, still making cooing noises.

MOTHER: We're all going for a walk together. Yes we are. Yes we are.

VIDEO: The five of them amble on out of camera range.

The Bear Cavalry – Page 183

VO: What the hell?

COMMENTS

Jess Morrow: I can't believe she handed her baby over to those things to eat.

Amatagat: Jesus Christ, Jess, you're a cynical bitch. Seek psychological help.

****

NINE YEARS LATER

SHARECROWS NEST - A MESSAGE BOARD

THOMAS: Hey, anyone seen that video of a mother handing her baby over to those things?

WIN: It's ancient. What is it, ten years old?

CAREGIRL: It's fake.

THOMAS: You don't know that.

CAREGIRL: It's been debunked. No one could find the mother or the baby. It's a hoax. All these videos popping up of Sharebears attacking humans, I'm not saying it doesn't happen. But most of these clips are faked, fake blood, edits, if you watch, it's all play behavior that people are misrepresenting.

THOMAS: Some of this looks pretty real.

CAREGIRL: I'm not denying that it's possible to get hurt. They're carnivores, they have teeth and claws, it's easy to get scratched or bitten by accident, if you're not careful, and most people aren't careful.

THOMAS: Accident, uh?

The Bear Cavalry – Page 184

CAREGIRL: Accident.

THOMAS: What about that woman in Detroit, they found her half eaten in her own home, the Sharebears were still chowing down when they found them. Human remains in their stomachs. Open and shut case.

CAREGIRL: Heart attack, the bears were stuck in there with her, the dead body was the only food source. There was no sign of a struggle or attack. We see dogs and cats doing the same thing when their shut in owner dies.

THOMAS: Bull.

CAREGIRL: There are very very few cases of Sharebears deliberately attacking or injuring a human being, almost none.

WIN: Because they 'love' us.

CAREGIRL: Yeah, they're friendly and affectionate, and they get along with people. But that's not it. If you can set aside your kneejerk hysteria, I'll explain it.

WIN: Explain away, professor.

CAREGIRL: It's very simple: We feed them. We feed them constantly, so they're never hungry around us. It's that hormonal thing they do, yes, it makes us like them and makes us want to feed them. As long as we keep shoving food at them, they're not interested in eating, or even attacking humans. It just doesn't happen.

THOMAS: Unless they feel like it.

CAREGIRL: Come on, this is just anthropomorphizing. They're not from outer space. They're not secret geniuses. They're not plotting together. They're just animals. They're just a version of skunks, but instead of a stinky toxic spray, they evolved a euphoric that didn't work particularly well in nature, so they evolved social behavior to compensate, and these traits just happens to serve them very well in human society. It's not magic.

THOMAS: Tell it to the cats and dogs.

WIN: What?

THOMAS: Where they start showing up, cat and dog populations start to drop.

CAREGIRL: Boo hoo, people are finding a better, more emotionally rewarding pet. That's competition in the marketplace. That's capitalism, boys.

THOMAS: Feral cats and dogs, and urban wildlife, raccoons, rats, you name it.

WIN: Anything that makes the rat population drop is a good thing.

THOMAS: You're pretty glib.

CAREGIRL: And you're over-reacting. I bet you haven't even met a sharebear up close. You should try it, you'd see how you're over-reacting.

THOMAS: I don't want to be any closer than a snipers rifle.

WIN: Amen!

CAREGIRL: Like that guy in Tucson? He shot a civilian, you know.

THOMAS: The civilian jumped in the way.

CAREGIRL: Like in the movies? Yeah, that's not how it works. In real life, bullets go really fast. He was a psycho, and he didn't care if he killed a few people.

THOMAS: Still...

CAREGIRL: I've seen them up close. They're not big deal. You can get a little goofy at first, but that's all. It's not like they're mind controlling you. Hell, I spent eight hours on a train with some. No ill effects.

THOMAS: Jesus. You mean to tell me you're a Sharer.

CAREGIRL: We don't like that word. We're not fanatics.

WIN: What the hell?

CAREGIRL: Look the ecology is out of whack, species everywhere are out of balance, there's no more natural order left. You act like it's a crime to reintroduce, or introduce species into a damaged ecosystem.

THOMAS: I can't believe this.

CAREGIRL: Yeah, well, if we don't do something pro-active, there isn't going to be an ecosystem left. Then what are you paranoid conspiracy theorists going to do?

****

FOURTEEN YEARS LATER

SHARECROWS NEST - A MESSAGE BOARD

AL: There was another plane crash.

JEN: Oh cripes, not this again.

MOD: Al, is this another conspiracy theory? Because this is your third warning. Your privileges are about to be revoked.

AL: Haven't you noticed the last ten years, more plane crashes every year, more accidents, more malfunctions.

JEN: Here it comes. Goodbye Al, it was nice knowing you.

The Bear Cavalry – Page 187

AL: At the same time, their population has skyrocketed. They're everywhere now. They're all over the place. Remember when we used to argue about whether they would attack a person. Now, its official, they eat winos.

KEVIN: Who cares about winos? Remember when everyone was always pissing about the homeless? Remember the crime that came with the homeless? The losers, the addicts, the bunch of them? They don't bother people that can look after themselves. It's just nature, man, and you can't blame them for being natural.

JEN: Nature's law trumps man's law.

AL: And there's cases documented where they'll go into an only child household, and kill the child, and the family just starts to revolve around them.

JEN: Yeah, that's ugly, and we should watch out for that. We should be making sure that the child can co-exist, that he's not a threat to the sharebear so it doesn't have to react defensively.

AL: No, that's not acceptable. Ten years ago, people would have been freaking out about this, people would have been going nuts. Now it's 'who cares about winos' and 'too bad about the kids.'

JEN: That was offensive. I didn't say 'too bad about the kids.' You're not being fair.

AL: Things are changing, and we don't even notice. It's like we're frogs in water that's slowly being brought to a boil, and we just keep sitting there.

JEN: I disagree.

AL: There's studies linking their euphorics with long term cognitive breakdown, permanent neurological changes. As little as one or two exposures and we're seeing long term behavior changes. And no one is paying attention!

KEVIN: A lot of those studies are exaggerated. You can't trust everything you read. These alarmists, man, they have an agenda they're pushing.

AL: The agenda is not being eaten.

JEN: Al, give it a break. We've heard all these exaggerations before, you're like a broken record.

AL: There's more of them around in urban centers than ever before, and they've been around for a long time now. There's evidence their euphorics persist in the environment. No one knows what those concentrations are doing. And we've got planes dropping out of the sky.

KEVIN: I'm not following you. Are you saying that it's causing airplanes to fall apart.

AL: No, I'm saying that euphorics are in the environment, and people aren't as careful, error rates go up, planes fall out of the sky, surgeons make mistakes, mechanics make mistakes, drivers... people are dying.

KEVIN: You're saying that because of Sharebears, people are on the whole happier, and that's a bad thing? Geez, you're delusional on so many levels.

AL: We used to be afraid of sharks. Leopards. Lions. Tigers. Wolves. Saber Tooth Tigers, Cave Bears. In the end, we beat them all. Nothing could touch us. We were the dominant species. But I think we've found a predator that figured out a way to use us against ourselves, and we have no defense. Their weapon wasn't teeth or claws, it was love and hugs, and we fall for it. We can't stop ourselves from falling for it.

MOD: Final warning, Al.

The Bear Cavalry – Page 189

AL: What happens to prey, when there's a predator that it has no defense against? A predator that we can't kill, because it makes us want to protect it. Everywhere I look, the world is falling apart around me, and no one seems to care. It's not that the evidence isn't there, the studies the predictions, the graphs. No one cares. What's the world going to be like in another ten years? Or five?

MOD: Banned from the list, conspiracy theory and negativity. Goodbye Al. Have a nice life. And for god's sakes, hug a bear, maybe you'll be able to stand yourself.

END

A Note From the Author

First up, I want to thank you for taking the time out to read my little book. If you've made it all the way here, then I'm just going to assume you liked it. Anyway, was a hoot to write, and the research was fascinating. Also a shout out to Christopher Martinez, my cover artist, who did a wonderful job.

If you've skipped to the end, looking for an apology, well... Sorry. Also: No refunds.

But anyway, I just wanted to say that I appreciate you're buying this, If you liked this, could I suggest you leave a review online or wherever you got it. Mention it on your blog, or your Facebook. Say nice things. If that's too much, just toss me a couple of stars. Writing is a solitary, lonely pursuit and actually getting some feedback or appreciation is a wonderful thing.

But there's more to it. It's about trying to get out there. There are a lot of people writing a lot of books, and it can get hard to get noticed. Reviews help. A casual browser who finds a book has been given stars, or reviews, they're more likely to take a chance and buy the book. The more books I sell, the happier I am, and the more I can write. Presumably that's a good thing. So help a guy out.

And speaking of writing more....

FUNNY FANTASY
And COMIC SCIENCE FICTION

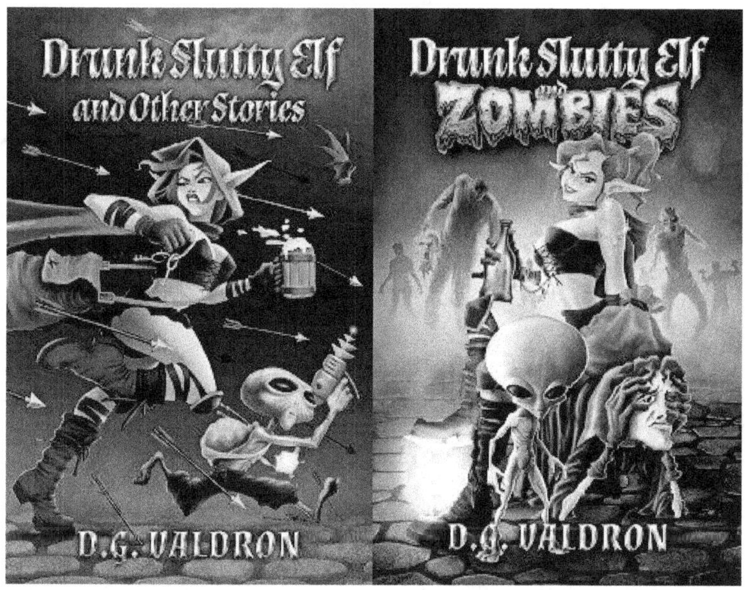

DRUNK SLUTTY ELF AND OTHER STORIES
Plus
DRUNK SLUTTY ELF AND ZOMBIES

Two volumes of savage, satirical, subversive wicked, funny, frantic science fiction and fantasy. Demented ghost hunters, frustrated aliens, horny giants, drunken elves, sneaky ghosts, wayward barbarians and many more.

ALTERNATE REALITIES
A Trilogy or Strange New Worlds
The Other books

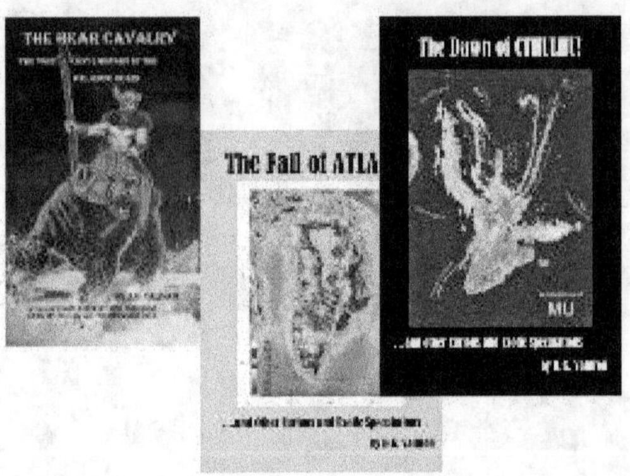

First up is the companion volume, a collection called **The Dawn of Cthulhu** - The Secret History of H.P. Lovecraft's Cthulhu Cult, from the Egyptian High Kingdom, to the present day. Lost Continents Found an exploration of mythical and actual sunken continents. The Monsters of Sesame Street, Muppets as if they were actual animals.

The Fall of Atlantis includes a geo-historical exploration of a real Atlantis ending in a different kind of tragedy; the Retoverse, a fun the accidental cinematic universe of 50s sci fi films, Ancient Rome plausibly crossing the Atlantic, because of coffee(!!!), and the saga of an Alternate Greenland that was never covered by ice.

AXIS OF ANDES
NEW WORLD WAR
A History of WWII in South America

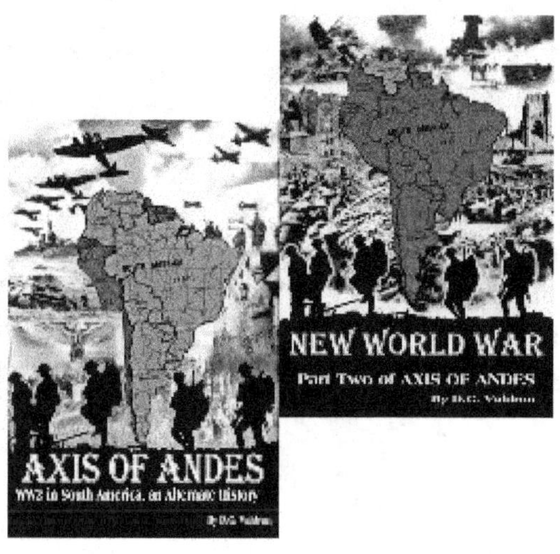

Berlin, 1937, Adolph Hitler and his cabinet meet with a strange delegation from Ecuador. The delegates from the small South American nation beg for help, fearing an impending invasion from their rival, Peru. What happens at that meeting sets in motion a chain of events that sets the entire continent on fire. By the time it's done, millions are dead, nations are in ruins, and the map of Latin America will be changed beyond recognition.

HEARTS IN DARKNESS
Three Collections of Horror Stories

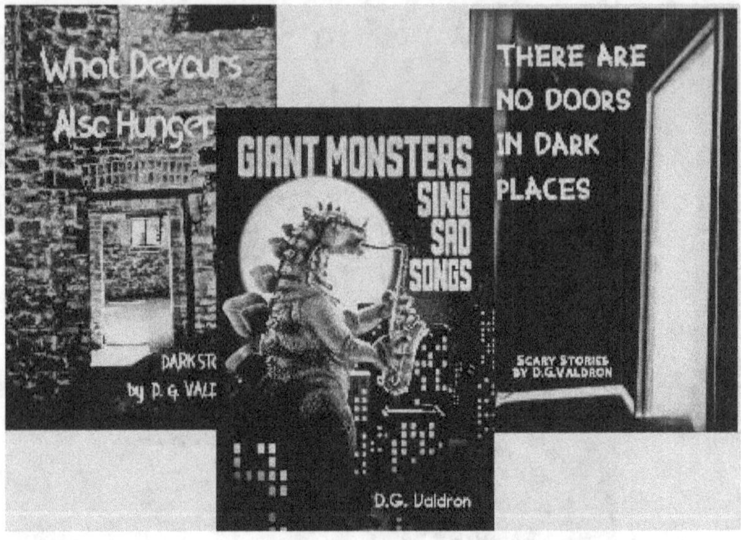

Featuring riveting stories about a man's cancer learning to talk to him, the ultimate serial killer; Allison, a paralyzed pregnant woman feeling her fetus taking control of her body, a desperate singl mother lured down a dark path; the army enlisting the unkillable men in the masks; Silence about a thief hiding in the home of a killer; a ghost that haunts the people around its victim, and many, many more. Melancholy darkness, chilling horror, dark visions.

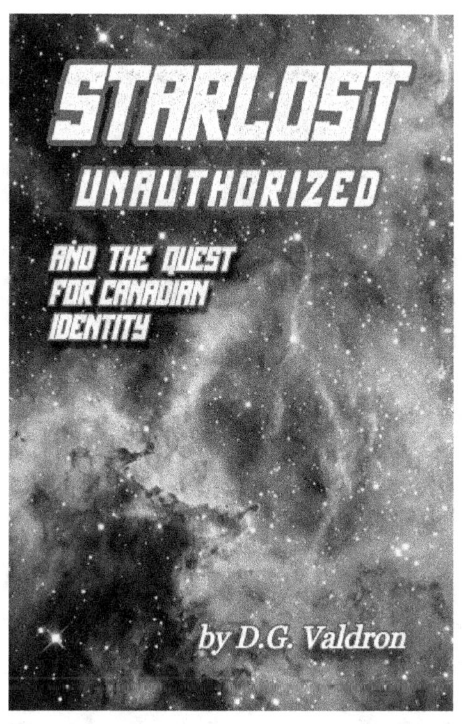# STARLOST UNAUTHORIZED

And the Quest for Canadian Identity

The series that was Harlan Ellison's nemesis. The most controversial series in the history of sci fi television. This exhaustively researched book, based on interviews with some of the stars and writers, brings a fresh new interpretation of of the Starlost, and a re-evaluation of the series and its themes in the context of the 1970s crisis of Canadian nationalism.

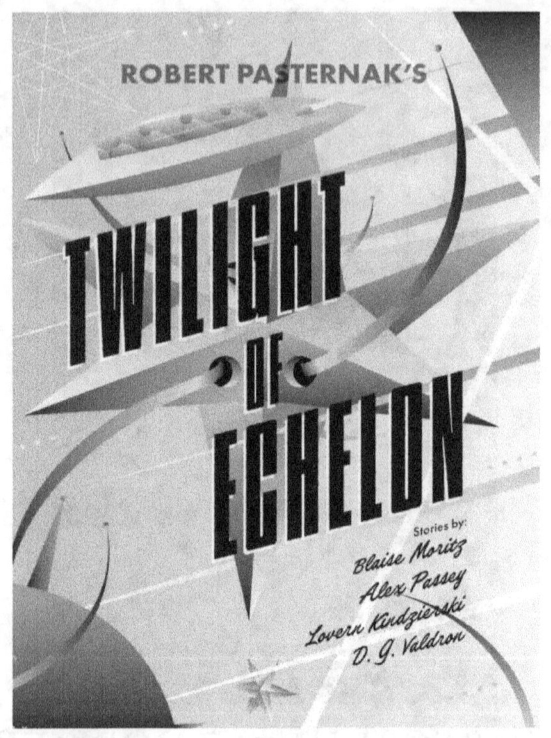

TWILIGHT OF ECHELON

Published by AT BAY PRESS

Based on the work of famed artist Robert Pasternak the book features paintings from Pasternak's Echelon series, accompanied by stories written independently by D.G. Valdron, Lovern Kindzierski, Alex Passey and Blaise Moritz.

A Pirates History of Doctor Who

The greatest, most professional Doctor Who fan films ever made, explorations of the peculiarities of copyright, the developments of new technologies, the evolution of fan culture, and histories of the Doctor on stage, in audio, and in animation. These books are full of new and entertaining insights and revelations that you'll love.

The Bear Cavalry – Page 198

LEXX UNAUTHORIZED

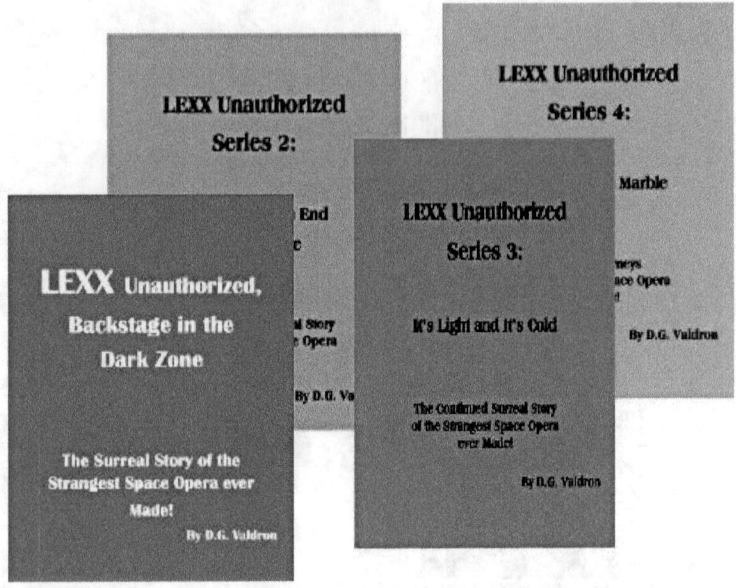

LEXX a show about a giant space bug that blows up planets, the cowardly security guard who is its captain, and the undead assassin, runaway love slave, and robot head who form its crew.

Originally billed as **'Star Trek's Evil Twin,'** the cultiest of cult sci fi, LEXX's forte was black humor, startling visuals, big ideas, and a sensibility that had more to do with surrealists like Jodorowsky or Bunuel than mainstream science fiction. And, as unconventional as it was onscreen, the story of how it came to be is even more bizarre.

The Bear Cavalry – Page 199

A Dark Fantasy
of Murder and Redemption

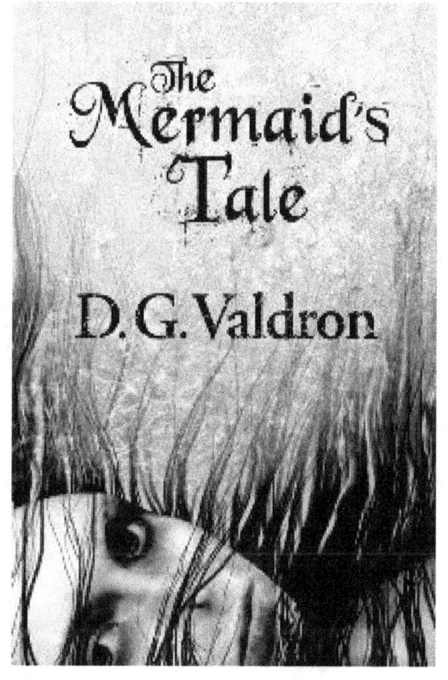

There's a City where all the races come together uneasily.

There's a Civil War gathering, and dark powers assembling.

There's a Mermaid, murdered cruelly her people distraught.

There's an Orc, lowest and the worst, assigned to solve the murder, before it all comes crashing down.

And there's something else, this world's first serial killer.

The Bear Cavalry – Page 200